Match Wits with Super Sleuth Nancy Drew!

Collect the Original
Nancy Drew Mystery Stories®
by Carolyn Keene

Available in Hardcover!

Celebrate 60 Years with the World's Best Detective!

THE HAUNTED BRIDGE

Mr. Drew is on the trail of an international ring of jewel thieves and asks Nancy to assist him: The trail leads to a summer resort area. Before Nancy has a chance to start work on her father's case, a golf caddy tells her a frightening tale. In the dense woods nearby is an old wooden footbridge guarded by a ghost! Intrigued by the caddy's story, Nancy decides to investigate.

Several riddles confront the young detective as she attempts to solve the mystery of the haunted bridge and track down a woman suspected of being a key member of the gang of jewel thieves.

How Nancy finds the answers to the two mysteries and at the same time, despite her injured hand, wins a trophy in a golf tournament will thrill all Nancy Drew fans.

Ned placed the paper in the hand of the marble figure

The Haunted Bridge

BY CAROLYN KEENE

GROSSET & DUNLAP
Publishers • New York
A member of The Putnam & Grosset Group

PRINTED ON RECYCLED PAPER

Acknowledgement is made to Mildred Wirt Benson, who under the pen name
Carolyn Keene, wrote the original NANCY DREW books

Contents

The Haunted
Bridge

CHAPTER I

Invitation to Mystery

"SORRY, miss, but I wouldn't go near that bridge for a million dollars," said the young, freckle-faced caddy.

"Why, Chris?" Nancy Drew asked him.

She had just driven her golf ball over two hundred yards into a patch of woods bordering the sixteenth hole. A rustic footbridge stood at the far side of it.

"Because the place is haunted, that's why."

Nancy, a slender attractive girl of eighteen with reddish-blond hair, was intrigued. She requested more details. Before Chris could answer, the other girls who were in Nancy's threesome walked toward her with their caddies.

"What's up?" asked George Fayne, a trim-looking brunette with short hair and a boyish name.

"The bridge in there has a ghost guarding it," Chris replied. "Isn't that right, fellows?"

The other caddies nodded and cast wary glances among the trees.

The third girl, blond, pretty Bess Marvin, gasped. "A—a real ghost?"

"That's right, miss," Chris told her. "You'd better not hang around here."

Nancy smiled. "What will the ghost do to me?"

"Who knows?" Chris retorted, and started to move off. "He sure wouldn't let you take your ball, and he might strike you. Come on! Take a penalty stroke."

"I guess we'd better," Bess agreed. "There's a foursome right behind us. Shall I signal them to play through?"

"No, we may as well go on," Nancy decided.

Her caddy was obviously relieved. "You couldn't have played from behind all those trees, anyway," he said.

"It's a shame," George commented. "You had such a great score up to now, Nancy. I hate to see you lose a stroke."

Nancy's curiosity about the haunted bridge distracted her attention from the game, and she scored a disappointing double bogey for the hole.

"Oh, you should have had a par," George murmured sympathetically.

Nancy smiled. "I've learned never to count my score until the last hole is played."

Nancy smiled. "What will the ghost do to me?"

"You'll certainly qualify for the tournament," Bess insisted. "That is, if you don't let your mind wander off on the mystery."

The three girls were spending a few weeks at the Deer Mountain Hotel as guests of Nancy's father, Carson Drew. He had come there on legal business. The summer resort with its many sports activities was a contrast to the comparative quiet of River Heights, their hometown, and the girls were enjoying every minute of the vacation.

Before their arrival, Mr. Drew had hinted that he might ask Nancy to aid him with a puzzling case he was handling. As yet, he had not explained what the work involved. During the lawyer's lengthy absences from the hotel the girls had been swimming and playing tennis and golf.

George and Bess thoroughly enjoyed golf. Both played well, but it was Nancy's scores which had attracted the attention of the club's golf pro. He had urged her to enter the qualifying round of an important championship tournament for amateur golfers to be held shortly.

Nancy felt she could offer little competition to the excellent women players at the hotel. But Bess and George had persuaded her to try out and finally she had consented.

"You'll bring home the trophy, Nancy!" George declared as the girls finished playing the seventeenth hole.

When they approached the eighteenth tee they

noticed that another player was there ahead of them. He was a tall, thin man in his late twenties, immaculately dressed in white slacks. Bushy black hair and a beard partially covered his angular, hard face.

"Oh, he's Martin Bartescue," Nancy said in an undertone. "Let's slow up."

The warning was too late. Bartescue had seen the girls. He waved and waited for them to approach.

"We would have to run into *him!*" Bess commented in disgust.

Martin Bartescue had met the girls the previous evening and immediately he had tried to make a golfing date with Nancy. Although she had heard the man was a very good player, she had taken an instant dislike to him, and politely declined the invitation.

Obviously he liked to brag, and she doubted the truth of his many stories of being friends with famous people. Now, as the girls seated themselves on a bench directly behind the driving area, he did not tee off. Instead, Bartescue smiled and walked over to them.

"May I have the honor of playing in with you young ladies?" he asked engagingly.

"We may as well all walk together," Nancy replied politely but with no warmth in her voice.

She drove a long, straight ball, while Bess and George played somewhat shorter ones down the fairway. Bartescue's drive outdistanced Nancy's. As the group moved along, he walked beside her.

"You play a fine game, Nancy," he said. "I was just thinking that you might like to enter the mixed foursome tournament with me next week. Together we should win first place."

"I may not be here that long," Nancy replied.

Bartescue looked disappointed. "I've played golf courses all over the world," he boasted. "Once I played the Prince of Wales."

"And did you defeat him?" Nancy asked, trying to hide a smile.

"Well, yes, I did," Bartescue admitted. "But only by a couple of strokes. Oh, I've often played with royalty."

By this time Nancy had reached her ball. When she was about to hit it, Bartescue stepped closer. His movement distracted her as she took her backswing. As a result, she dubbed the shot.

"Too bad, too bad," he muttered sympathetically. "You pulled in your elbow just as you struck the ball. Here, let me show you."

He took the club from the girl's hand, and to the annoyance of the trio insisted upon giving a demonstration of what he considered to be Nancy's fault. Without commenting on his criticism, Nancy walked to her ball and, in her usual good form, hit a beautiful shot down the middle of the fairway.

"That's fine." Bartescue nodded. "You'll make a par five on this hole, the way the pros do."

Determined to play her best, Nancy approached the eighteenth green. Her ball was only five feet from the cup. Intensely annoyed because Bartescue was still offering advice, she stepped up to putt. The ball rolled in a straight line toward the cup and came to a stop at the very edge of it.

"Oh, Nancy! What a shame!" Bess wailed.

Immediately Bartescue jumped up and down on the ground. The vibration caused the ball to drop into the cup.

"There, Nancy! You made a par five."

"That wasn't fair, Mr. Bartescue," she said severely. "I'll add an extra putt which gives me a six."

"But why? You didn't strike the ball."

The girls smiled coldly. Murmuring a few polite phrases, they left the man staring blankly after them and walked to the hotel.

"Of all the conceited people!" Bess exclaimed when they were beyond Bartescue's range of hearing. "I'll bet he never came within a mile of royalty, to say nothing of defeating the Prince of Wales by a couple of strokes!"

"And he made you miss your shot, Nancy," George stated irritably.

"You'll surely qualify, anyway," Bess said as she studied the scorecards. "George has an eighty-five. My score is a disgraceful ninety, but, Nancy, you have a brilliant seventy-five!"

"I wonder what became of my caddy," Nancy said. "I forgot to pay Chris. Also I wanted to question him about the haunted bridge."

"I suppose you'll want to inspect it," Bess said. "Well, if there's anything spooky about it, count me out when you investigate it."

"Do you think there's something to what Chris said?" George put in.

Nancy shrugged and replied, "I'm going to talk to him and find out more about the mystery of the haunted bridge!"

Before the girls had a chance to search for Chris, Bartescue approached them in the hotel lobby.

"Oh, I wonder if you'd like to attend—"

"Not just now," Nancy said quickly. "I must find my caddy."

"I'll go with you—" the man began, but Nancy pretended not to hear him and excused herself.

She retraced her steps to the eighteenth green. Though several caddies were lingering nearby, hers was not among them. She questioned another boy about him.

"Chris is just starting out with a twosome," he said. "You might catch him at the first tee."

Nancy thanked the boy and hastened to the starting point, which was hidden from her view by a wing of the Deer Mountain Hotel. Two men had just teed off. As she approached them she observed Chris starting down the fairway behind the players.

"Oh, Chris, just a minute," Nancy hailed him. "I forgot to pay you," she added with a smile, taking some money from her pocket. "I want to ask you about that haunted bridge."

"I can't stop to talk now," the boy replied.

"I understand. But will you meet me near the caddy house after you've finished work?" Nancy requested. "About five o'clock?"

"I'll be there," Chris promised.

He hurried off, and Nancy slowly made her way back to the hotel lobby where she found Bess and George talking to Martin Bartescue. He was telling them about the many prominent persons with whom he was acquainted.

"I believe I'll turn my scorecard in to the tournament chairman now," Nancy remarked to the girls. "If one of you will attest it—"

"Here, allow me," interrupted Bartescue. Before Nancy could prevent him, he had taken the scorecard.

As he signed his name, Nancy noted a rather curious thing. It seemed to her that he formed each letter with painful precision. Why? Was he trying to disguise his handwriting?

CHAPTER II

Unlucky Fall

NANCY took her scorecard from Martin Bartescue and walked on with Bess and George. Knowing the card had to be signed by someone accompanying her throughout the game, she asked George to attest the score. Then Nancy gave the card to the tournament chairman who was in his office busily chalking up the results of the day's matches.

"A fine score, Miss Drew," he praised her.

"Do you think she will qualify for the tournament?" Bess asked the man eagerly.

"She certainly will unless better scores come in tomorrow," he replied with a smile. "However, the competition is very keen this year. Some of the best women golfers in the state are entering the tournament."

"I'll feel very fortunate if I so much as qualify," Nancy replied. "I understand there's to be a tournament for men, too."

"Yes, I have entered it," said a voice behind the girls. They glanced around to find Bartescue standing there. "So far my score is the lowest turned in," he added.

"That's great," Nancy murmured indifferently, hurrying away with her friends.

As the girls took the elevator to their rooms on the fourth floor, Bess and George teased Nancy about her new admirer.

"You're stuck with him," George prophesied.

"I dislike his type and you both know it," Nancy replied. "But one thing about him did capture my interest."

Bess giggled. "What was that? His ultramodern clothes?"

"Oh, Bess, of course not," Nancy said. "I was interested in the way he signed my scorecard. Did you notice how unnaturally he wrote his signature, as if he were trying to disguise his usual style of writing?"

"Why, no," George admitted in surprise. "You seem to observe everything, Nancy."

"I guess that's why she has solved so many baffling mysteries." Bess sighed. "Nancy knows how to make use of her eyes and we don't."

"Dad trained me to be observant," Nancy said.

As the girls started down the hall toward their rooms, she thought proudly of her father, Carson Drew, whose fame as a criminal lawyer was nationwide. Through helping him, Nancy herself had achieved distinction. She was now a well-known amateur detective with a long list of successful mystery cases to her credit, the most recent one *The Whispering Statue.*

Nancy's father was very proud of her too. Mrs. Drew had died when Nancy was only three years old. Since then their home had been managed by lovable Hannah Gruen, an excellent housekeeper.

Thinking of the woman who had cared for her like a mother, Nancy smiled. "Can you imagine what Hannah would say if she knew I was starting another mystery?"

"She'd say, 'Now, Nancy, promise you'll be careful!'" Bess replied with a grin.

Laughing, the three entered the cousins' big, comfortably furnished bedroom.

"Speaking of the mystery," said George, "did you learn anything about the haunted bridge?"

"Not yet," Nancy answered, glancing at her wrist watch. "But I'm to meet Chris at five."

Nancy found him waiting for her at the caddy house. He made no comment as she led him to a bench at the rear of the hotel.

"Please tell me everything you know about that bridge," she urged him. "Why do you say it's haunted?"

"Because it is," the boy insisted. "All the caddies will tell you the same. Sometimes you can see the ghost walking over it."

"At night?"

"Daytime, too. It waves its arms slowly back and forth. And sometimes the ghost screams as if it's in pain."

"Have you actually seen and heard this yourself?"

"Sure. That's why I know better than to go into that woods."

"You mean you've never been up close to the ghost?" Nancy inquired, smiling.

The boy frowned and said, "You couldn't hire any of the guys to go near the place."

"Chris, are the bridge and surrounding property owned by the hotel?" Nancy asked.

Before Chris could reply, the caddy master appeared to inform the boy he was wanted immediately in the caddy house.

"I'll have to go now," Chris told Nancy.

"Thank you for telling me about the ghost," she said. "And by the way, if I qualify, would you like to caddy for me in the tournament?"

"Sure. But I won't promise to look for any balls in the woods."

Nancy leisurely walked back to the hotel. As she went through the lobby a sudden thought occurred to her. After giving a brief explanation, she asked the desk clerk if she might look at the registration cards of recent guests.

"Certainly, Miss Drew. Glad to be of help at any time."

Nancy flicked through the file until she came

to the name Martin Bartescue and studied the man's handwriting.

"It's not a bit like his signature on my score-card," she reflected.

Nancy was so absorbed in looking at it that she failed to observe the man himself. He had come up directly behind her. Pausing, he regarded her intently for a moment, then dodged into a telephone booth. Nancy, unaware of his presence, went upstairs.

Bess and George were dressing for dinner. They were not too occupied, though, to bombard Nancy with questions concerning the haunted bridge.

"I didn't learn much more except that the ghost walks across the bridge, not only at night, but also in the daytime."

Bess gave a nervous giggle. "I'll never let my ball go into that woods, even if I have to take ten iron shots on the fairway."

Nancy and George laughed. Then Nancy said, "Here's a new mystery. Bartescue uses at least two different styles of handwriting." She told about the registration cards.

"And probably several aliases," George commented with a look of disgust. "Anyway, hereafter I'm going to call him Barty."

"Barty the Barge-In!" Bess said.

That evening Mr. Drew had dinner with the

girls. Nancy noticed that her tall, handsome father seemed a bit preoccupied.

"Isn't your case progressing well, Dad?" she asked.

"Not so far," he replied. "I'll probably need your help soon, Nancy."

"I'll be ready."

After dinner Mr. Drew told the girls that he must leave the hotel for a few hours.

"We'll manage to amuse ourselves," Bess said, chuckling.

The hotel orchestra was an excellent one. The girls met many attractive young men who were vacationing at Deer Mountain. Nancy, Bess, and George were never at a loss for partners. Bartescue was persistent and danced with Nancy several times. Though he was an excellent dancer, Nancy did not enjoy being with him.

At the end of one number he firmly steered her toward the terrace. She was annoyed, but told herself, "This might be a chance to find out more about the man."

He launched into a story of his adventures in England. But at the first opportunity Nancy led him on to the subject that was uppermost in her mind.

"Obviously golf is one of your main interests, Mr. Bartescue. Do you also have other interests?"

"Oh, yes," he replied. "I enjoy tennis— But what are some of yours?"

"Well, for one thing, graphology intrigues me. Some people profess to be able to tell a person's character by means of his handwriting."

In the semidarkness she did not notice her companion regard her shrewdly as he answered, "What an interesting story could be built up around mine! The way I write varies with my moods. Today your charm had me so baffled I could hardly sign my name at all. I doubt that I would even recognize it on your scorecard."

Nancy glanced quickly at the man but his face was a mask. Unexpectedly he began to move closer.

"Nancy, you are very attractive. In all my life, I've never met anyone that I—"

Nancy took a step backward. She did not realize that she had been standing near the edge of the terrace. Suddenly her heels were no longer on solid cement and she felt herself falling. She gave a cry of alarm. Before Bartescue could extend a hand to save her she toppled into a flower bed!

"Oh, I'm sorry," he said. "Are you hurt?" he asked anxiously, springing down to assist her.

Nancy slowly rose from the ground, trying to brush the dirt from her long dress.

"I think I've sprained my hand," she admitted.

"Shall I call a doctor?" Bartescue asked.

"No, no. I'll be all right. Just leave me here."

Nancy's outcry had brought several dancers running from the hotel ballroom. The situation was intensely embarrassing to her. She did not wish to explain that her fall from the terrace had been caused by trying to avoid Bartescue's unwelcome attentions.

"Let me see your hand," Bartescue urged. "I don't believe the sprain is a bad one."

Nancy ignored him. Walking away swiftly, she went directly to her room. The pain in her left hand was not so intense now, but the fingers were becoming stiff.

"I'll never be able to play in the tournament," she thought miserably.

While Nancy was in the bathroom running cold water on her hand, Bess and George came hurrying into the room.

"Oh, Nancy," Bess wailed, "we just heard about your accident. Barty said you weren't hurt, but you are!"

"Let me see the injury, Nancy," George demanded.

"There's nothing to see. The skin isn't even broken. But my hand still hurts!"

"You must go to a doctor," George urged.

At that moment Carson Drew returned to the hotel and came straight to his daughter's room. Upon hearing about the injury, he too became concerned, particularly when Nancy admitted that her back had been twisted slightly.

"Now don't be foolish," he said severely. "I'm going to have the house physician come up."

Dr. Aikerman was a quiet, dignified man who had little to say. The few words he spoke after his examination were directly to the point.

"This sprain isn't serious, but you must give your hand a rest. I'll bind it for you and don't use this hand for three or four days."

"You mean I can't play any golf?"

"No golf."

"But, Doctor," Nancy pleaded, "it really doesn't hurt very much. And the tournament starts day after tomorrow."

CHAPTER III

Nancy's Assignment

"NANCY stands a very good chance of participating in the tournament," Bess told the doctor. "It would be a shame if she couldn't play."

"Well," he said finally, after studying Nancy with twinkling eyes, "I suppose you could play. But right now I advise against it. However, by tomorrow night I may alter my opinion."

Dr. Aikerman picked up his physician's bag. "Nancy, I suggest a hot bath and a body massage to prevent your muscles from becoming stiff." The idea rather appealed to Nancy, who felt battered and sore.

After the doctor had gone, George spoke up, "Bess and I could give you a good rub."

Nancy regarded her dubiously.

"There's absolutely nothing to it," Bess put in. "You locate the various muscles and then rub until the soreness is all gone."

Nancy allowed herself to be persuaded. After the hot bath, she stretched herself full length on the bed.

"Where do you hurt the most?" George inquired.

"Everywhere." Nancy groaned. "Oh, don't rub in that spot, please, George. It's too tender!"

"I have to massage the muscles," her friend insisted.

"Where did you get that bottle of liniment?" Nancy demanded. "It smells awful."

"This is a free massage, so don't be so critical."

Bess relieved George when the latter's arms grew weary of the task. There was no rest or relaxation for Nancy. She was pummeled and pounded by her well-meaning but inexperienced masseuses until she felt ready to cry from sheer exhaustion.

"Oh, girls, I can't stand any more," she pleaded finally. "Just let me crawl under the covers and go to sleep."

"We're through now, anyway," Bess declared as she helped Nancy roll over on her back again. "In the morning you'll feel fine."

"I hope so."

Nancy closed her eyes. Before George could snap out the light, the telephone rang. Bess answered the call.

"It's for you, Nancy. Long distance."

"I wonder who it can be. I hope nothing is

wrong at home," Nancy said anxiously as she painfully pulled herself to a sitting position and took the phone.

A familiar voice at the other end of the line said cheerily, "Hello. Nancy? This is Ned. Can you hear me?"

"Perfectly. Hi!"

"Your voice doesn't sound natural," Ned Nickerson remarked. "I guess I shouldn't have bothered you so late at night. But I thought maybe you weren't having a very exciting time and would like to hear from an old friend, meaning me."

"Oh, Ned, I love hearing from you, but you're entirely wrong about there being no excitement at Deer Mountain."

She told him about the haunted bridge, her unpleasant experience with Martin Bartescue, and finally of the accident.

"I'd like to give that guy a going over he wouldn't forget!" Ned replied angrily.

"You can't very well do it by long distance." Nancy laughed.

"No, but you may be seeing me sooner than you expect. I thought if you were planning to stay at the hotel for several days I might drive up with a couple of buddies."

"Meaning Burt and Dave?" Nancy asked.

"Yes."

"Terrific, Ned! And before you come will you

do me a special favor? Would you look in the Social Register and see if Martin Bartescue is listed?"

"Say, I hope you're not getting interested in that—"

"Now don't be alarmed, Ned," Nancy interrupted. After explaining the situation, she hung up and told Bess and George the good news.

In the morning Nancy awoke feeling greatly refreshed. Her back was not so sore as she had expected, though her hand still hurt. She needed her friends' assistance to dress and had just slipped on her shoes when a telephone call came from Mr. Drew.

"How would you like to take a ride with me this morning? That is, if you feel all right."

"Of course. I'm much better," Nancy answered promptly.

Intuition told her that the ride might have something to do with her father's mysterious case.

"We girls will be down to breakfast in five minutes."

They were about to leave their rooms when a porter appeared with a box of flowers for Nancy. She assumed that her father had sent them. As Nancy tore away the tissue paper from a dozen red roses in a container, a card dropped to the floor. She picked it up.

"Martin Bartescue!" Nancy exclaimed as she

read the name. She left the flowers in the box and walked away.

"Wait a minute!" Bess cried out. "Even if you don't like the man, don't punish the poor flowers." She rescued the roses and got water for them in the bathroom. "I've never seen a more attractive arrangement."

"They are pretty," Nancy admitted reluctantly. "I suppose he sent them because he feels responsible for my falling off the terrace."

"Wear one of the roses down to breakfast," Bess suggested.

"I'd rather not, but you girls are welcome to them."

"No thanks," said George. "I don't like that man any better than you do."

"I don't either," Bess added.

Nancy looked at Bartescue's card once more. Turning it over, she saw that he had written a brief note of sympathy on the back.

"Girls, look at this handwriting!" she called.

"It's different from the signature on your scorecard," Bess observed.

"And from the one on the hotel registration card," Nancy told her.

George remarked, "I can't help but feel there's something suspicious about Martin Bartescue!"

Knowing that her father was waiting for her in the lobby, Nancy dropped the card into her

ithout further comment. The three girls
dly locked their doors and went downstairs.

irectly after breakfast Nancy and Mr. Drew
ove away. Bess and George decided to play tennis and do some letter writing.

While the Drews were riding along, the lawyer
revealed to his daughter that for the past week he
had been working on the legal angles of a smuggling case involving an international ring of jewel
thieves.

"It has baffled New York detectives. For many
months the customs authorities have been trying
to round up the gang. Now the work has spread
out all over the country. It's believed that one of
the members is a woman who frequents the summer resort hotels in this particular area. Unfortunately no description of her is available."

"Then how can you hope to trace her, Dad?"

"There is one good clue."

"What is that?"

"Detectives have learned that the woman car-
ries an expensive jeweled compact set with dia-
monds and precious stones. In the case is a small
picture of a child."

"Her own child?"

"I don't know, Nancy. There is very little information about this woman."

"And you say she frequents the better hotels
near here?"

"Yes. For days a woman detective who works

with me has been making the rounds, searching for her. Miss Ingle has been taken ill and will be in a hospital for a while. That brings me to the point of why I invited you to come with me, Nancy. How would you like to take Miss Ingle's place until she's well again?"

"I'd love it!" Nancy cried promptly. "When do I start work?"

"This morning," her father replied with a smile as he turned the car into a curving side road. It led toward an imposing hotel at the top of a high cliff.

Mr. Drew parked his car in the grounds of the Hotel Lincoln. As he walked slowly toward the entrance with his daughter, he explained what he wished her to do.

"Your work is very simple, Nancy. While I interview the hotel clerk, you are to wander about the lobby. Observe the women who pass through to see if any seems to act suspiciously or happens to pull out a compact similar to the one I described. She might be a member of the gang of jewel thieves."

"I'll also look in the powder room," Nancy promised. "A woman naturally would make use of her compact there."

At the hotel entrance Carson Drew said, "We'll separate now. Meet you in half an hour at the car."

The lobby was fairly crowded so Nancy at-

tracted no particular attention as she seated herself near the elevator. Here she could see everyone
who entered and left by the front door.

Presently, satisfied that the woman she sought
was not on the main floor, Nancy went upstairs
to look in the ladies' lounge. She saw several
women take compacts from their bags, but none
of the containers was jeweled.

The chimes of a clock warned Nancy that she
must return to the car to meet her father. "I
shouldn't keep him waiting."

"No luck?" Mr. Drew inquired, noting her unhappy expression.

"Absolutely none."

"Well, we're only beginning our search," he
remarked cheerfully, starting the engine. "An in-
vestigator's work is always tedious."

A short time later the lawyer drove the car into
the grounds of Hemlock Hall, a hotel even larger
and more exclusive than the Lincoln. "See you in
half an hour."

In the crowded lobby Nancy soon lost sight of
her father. She became completely absorbed in
her task of studying the women guests. Nancy was
a bit dismayed when she glanced at her wrist
watch. She must hurry if she were not to be late
meeting her father!

"I'll check out the powder room before I rejoin Dad," she said to herself.

The place was deserted, except for a maid and

an attractive-looking woman in her early twenties. Nancy gazed at the latter intently and immediately noted the sad expression on her face.

"She can't be the person I'm after," Nancy thought, and made a pretense of combing her hair before the mirror.

Her eyes were not upon her own reflection, but focused on the woman who sat nearby.

The next moment Nancy nearly dropped her comb as she saw the stranger open her handbag and take out a beautiful compact set with sparkling gems!

CHAPTER IV

A Weird Sight

NANCY's heart leaped with excitement. Had she found the person for whom her father was searching?

The woman raised her eyes, flushing slightly as she became aware of Nancy's stare.

"I don't mean to be rude," the young detective said, "but I couldn't help admiring your beautiful compact. I've never seen one like it."

The stranger graciously handed it to Nancy for closer inspection. With trembling fingers the young detective unfastened the catch. Would the case contain the picture of a child?

With mingled feelings of relief and disappointment, Nancy saw that the inside of the cover held only a mirror. After a few admiring comments, she returned the case, and asked the woman if she were a guest at the hotel.

"No, I'm not," the other admitted. "I came to

have lunch with a friend. Are you spending your vacation here?"

Nancy shook her head. "I'm staying at Deer Mountain Hotel."

"Lovely place," the young woman remarked. She paused as she powdered her face, then went on, "I formerly lived only a short distance from there. My home was destroyed by fire."

Before Nancy could inquire about the exact location of the house or the stranger's name, the woman arose. After replacing the compact in her bag, she left the room.

Nancy was tempted to follow her, but could think of no pretext for reopening the conversation. She returned to the car and found her father waiting for her.

"You're late, Nancy. We won't have time to visit another hotel. I must get back to Deer Mountain for an important interview."

"I'm sorry I took so long, Dad. I thought I had located the woman you're looking for."

Nancy gave a detailed description of the jeweled compact which had attracted her attention and related the conversation with the young woman.

"Every clue is worth investigating," Mr. Drew assured Nancy, "and it's possible this woman may not be so innocent as she seems."

At Deer Mountain Hotel father and daughter had a quick lunch in the grill, then parted. Nancy found her friends resting in their room after several hours of vigorous exercise playing tennis.

"You were gone such a long while we began to wonder what had happened to you," George said as Nancy threw herself down into an overstuffed chair. "Tired?"

"Oh, a little, and my hand is hurting me again."

"Golf scores have been coming in all day," Bess reported, "but the last we heard you were still in the upper group."

"There seems to be a lot of gossip in the hotel about your friend Barty," George remarked. "One of the golf players, the former state champ, practically accused him of cheating."

Bess put in teasingly, "While you were away, Nancy, he telephoned twice. We told him you'd be back about two o'clock."

Nancy sighed. "It's after that now so he'll probably be calling again. I don't want to talk to him. Let's go for a walk to the woods near the sixteenth fairway. I'd like to visit the haunted bridge."

At once Bess objected. "Oh, we shouldn't go there alone," she murmured nervously.

"Now don't be silly," George chided her cousin. "You know very well there are no ghosts. It's only a story, of course."

"Stories seldom originate out of nothing," Bess retorted quickly. "I know we'll get into trouble."

Nancy and George promised they would be

careful. Reluctantly Bess followed them out of the room. By the time the girls reached the woods Bess began to lose her fear and to share their zest for the adventure.

"The bridge is down by the ravine, remember," Nancy said.

"I can see something white among the trees," George replied.

"Maybe it's the ghost!" Bess exclaimed.

Nancy and George pushed on through the dense tangle of underbrush, with Bess bringing up the rear. They were close enough now to see the footbridge. It was old and in need of repairs.

Nancy, who was in the lead, halted abruptly. Through the trees she could see something white flapping. The next moment a moaning and a weird groaning filled the air.

Bess gasped in horror. "The bridge *is* haunted!" she cried. "You can see the ghost waving its arms! Nancy, let's get out of here!"

"Nonsense," said George. "It's probably only a piece of white cloth fluttering in the wind."

"It *might* be," Bess admitted, "but did you ever hear a piece of cloth moan and groan?"

Nancy started to reply but the words died in her throat.

From somewhere up the ravine to their left came a fearful cry that rose to a screeching crescendo, then faded away with a tremulous wail.

"What was that?" whispered Bess.

"Maybe some kind of wild animal," replied George uneasily.

"Perhaps," Nancy said doubtfully. "But what could it be? I don't think there's anything larger than deer in these woods."

For several minutes the three girls huddled together, listening for the weird sound to be repeated. Through the screen of trees they could still see the white, ghostlike object moving its arms slowly to and fro.

"Come on," Nancy urged. "We'll approach quietly and see if we can surprise the ghost."

Bess pleaded with her companions to give up the adventure, but they paid no attention.

Nancy, who was ahead of the others, moved stealthily forward through the woods, taking care not to step on twigs nor to make any sound which would betray her presence. Suddenly she halted and began to laugh.

"Girls, Chris's so-called ghost is nothing but an old scarecrow!"

Moving slightly aside, Nancy pointed toward the bridge directly below. The girls were now close enough to see a tall, tattered white figure flapping in the breeze.

"That was a good joke on us!" George grinned.

No longer afraid, they hastened down into the ravine to examine the scarecrow. It had been set up at the entrance to the narrow, rustic footbridge that spanned a creek. Evidently the figure had been standing there for many months, because the white clothing was grimy and torn, and straw stuffing protruded from the shirt.

"The scarecrow is so wobbly," said George, "that the slightest breeze, or any vibration of the bridge causes it to move."

"Seeing the movement from a distance, I suppose the caddies imagined the figure was crossing the bridge," Nancy added.

"Well, I guess the mystery of the haunted bridge is solved," concluded George.

"How do you explain the moaning and the groaning we heard?" Bess asked. "Did we imagine it?"

"No," Nancy answered gravely. "Those noises were very real, and so was that terrible cry up the ravine. And we know none of them came from this scarecrow!"

"You don't suppose we heard the creaking of the bridge as it swayed in the wind?" Bess asked.

"No," Nancy replied. "It's possible some prankster may be at work around here. Let's make a search."

After the girls had investigated the area carefully they were more bewildered than before. There was no evidence of footprints in the vicinity of the bridge. Apparently no one had been there recently.

"Nobody's around here now," Nancy observed,

"but of course someone must have set up the scarecrow. But why?"

"There are no fruit trees nearby and no crops to be protected from crows," Bess commented. "It seems pretty obvious that someone wants to keep people from crossing the bridge."

"Shall we go to the other side?" Nancy asked.

"The bridge doesn't look safe to me," Bess protested.

"I think it will hold me," Nancy said. As she cautiously stepped onto the bridge, the rickety boards creaked.

Bess shuddered. "Oh, Nancy, please don't go any farther!" she cried. "There's nothing to see on the other side."

The young detective, her hands clenched around the wooden railing, edged her way to the middle of the bridge. Beads of perspiration dotted her forehead as the shaky supports swayed. Suddenly the railing billowed outward.

Bess and George gasped as Nancy paused, then deftly pulled the railing toward her. "Please turn back!" Bess called. "Let's look for your golf ball instead."

Nancy did not want to upset her friends and gingerly made her way back to them. "I'd very much like to find that ball," she said. "It's a prize one of mine. Jimmy Harlow, the champion, autographed it for me."

The girls poked among the bushes and leaves

for nearly fifteen minutes but could not locate the lost ball.

"Maybe it rolled into the creek," Bess suggested.

Nancy, who wore a pair of sturdy shoes, scrambled down the muddy bank. After a brief search she realized she was accomplishing nothing and was ruining her shoes. She decided to rejoin her friends who were watching from above. She walked along the edge of the creek looking for a place where the bank was not so steep.

Suddenly her eyes lighted upon a metal object half buried in thick mud. Excitedly Nancy stooped to pick it up.

CHAPTER V

Exciting Discovery

"Is that your ball, Nancy?" George called.

"No, it's a piece of brass. I think I've found an old plate!"

"A brass plate!" Bess exclaimed in wonder.

Meanwhile Nancy had pried the object out of the mud and saw that it was not a plate but a small carved chest.

"It looks valuable!" she gasped, holding up the article for Bess and George to see. "And it's very heavy."

"Nancy, you certainly were born lucky," George remarked. "You lose a golf ball and find a treasure chest!"

"This feels heavy enough to contain gold," Nancy declared, turning the curious object over in her two hands.

She estimated that the little chest was not more than six inches in length. It appeared to be approximately four inches wide and slightly less in depth.

"Open it quickly," Bess urged when Nancy rejoined them.

"The chest seems to be locked."

"Maybe the lid's stuck," George added. "Let me try." She had no better success.

"It's locked, all right," Bess declared. "We could try to smash the lid with a rock."

"Brass isn't easy to crack," Nancy replied. "Besides, I don't want to ruin such an attractive little chest. It will be beautiful when cleaned and polished."

"I'm curious to know what's inside," George interjected. "Any ideas, Nancy?"

"Maybe something valuable. The thing that interests me is, how did it get here—so close to the haunted bridge?"

"Perhaps the scarecrow put it there on his off-duty hours!" Bess suggested with a grin.

"Ha-ha. Very funny," her cousin answered. "Sounds like your brain has gone off duty."

Bess ignored the comment and remarked, "I'll bet the water washed it down here. The creek evidently was much higher at one time than it is now."

"I wonder," said Nancy, "if someone deliberately buried the chest—possibly the person who set up the scarecrow."

"Well, it's too deep a mystery for me," Bess

declared as the girls climbed out of the ravine with their treasure. "Nancy, if you can find the answer to this riddle you'll be good!"

"I mean to try at least," the young detective replied with a laugh.

The three girls soon emerged from the woods. They met no one as they cut across the golf course. But as they approached Deer Mountain Hotel they saw Martin Bartescue on the terrace. He sat sipping a cool drink under an umbrella at a table. He quickly arose and came toward the girls.

Nancy was annoyed. "That pest will be certain to see the chest and ask a million questions about it!" she murmured.

Bess, who was carrying a sweater, carefully tossed it over Nancy's arm so the object was concealed completely.

Before Bartescue could speak, Nancy said hastily, "Thank you for the beautiful flowers."

"You liked the roses?" He beamed. "I ordered the best I could get. Of course the florist shop here at Deer Mountain is not like those in New York or Europe. How are you feeling today?"

"Very well, except for my hand. One finger is still pretty useless," Nancy replied.

"Do you plan to play in the tournament?"

"Yes, if the doctor says I may, and providing I qualify."

Bartescue smiled. "Your score was one of the lowest turned in. You qualified easily."

"I was hoping to," she said. "Are you competing in the men's tournament tomorrow?"

"Oh yes, and I'm counting on winning the cup!" Bartescue announced. "I went out for a practice round this morning and shot a sixty-nine. I'm just coming into my game," he boasted. "I doubt if anyone here will be a match for me unless I go into an unexpected slump."

The girls found his bragging decidedly distasteful, but listened politely.

"May I treat you to ice cream?" he said as the four reached the hotel entrance. He seemed offended when Nancy declined.

When the girls gained the privacy of their adjoining bedrooms, Bess chuckled. "At least he didn't see the brass chest."

Nancy immediately tried to pry open the chest with a nail file but the lid would not budge.

"We need something with a sharp point," George declared as she studied the little chest. "If only we had an ice pick or something with a—"

Nancy sprang to her feet, her eyes full of excitement.

"Why didn't I think of it before?"

Without waiting to explain, she dropped the chest into George's lap and ran from the room.

She hurried through the hotel lobby to find a

tool with which to pry open the lid. As Nancy passed the flower shop, she paused a moment to admire the beautiful display in the window.

"It would be nice for me to send Bess and George each a bouquet," she mused. "They admired mine so much. They should have some of their own." She grinned.

Impulsively Nancy entered the shop, where she purchased two bouquets to be delivered immediately to her friends.

"Shall I include your name?" the clerk inquired politely.

"No, just write 'From A Friend.'"

Nancy knew that Bess and George would recognize her handwriting and thought it would be fun to tease them. She watched as the clerk wrote the message on two cards. Nancy picked up one and looked at it curiously.

"Your handwriting looks familiar," she said.

"I sometimes write cards for my customers. Did someone send you flowers from my shop?"

"Yes, I received a dozen roses from a man named Martin Bartescue."

"Oh, are you Miss Drew?"

"Yes, I am."

"I wrote the card that went with your flowers," the clerk recalled. "Mr. Bartescue requested me to do so."

"I see," Nancy murmured, without disclosing

by her tone that the information had special significance. She paid for the flowers and left.

As she passed the registration desk, the hotel clerk motioned to her. "Miss Drew, the tournament chairman asked me to give you this," he said and handed her a sealed envelope. To her delight, it contained an invitation to enter the official competition.

Excitedly Nancy hurried on to the caddy house, where her golf bag and spiked shoes were. Bess and George were mystified when their friend returned to the cousins' room holding the shoes and an envelope.

"Sharp gear!" Bess quipped. "What do you intend to do with those?"

Nancy laughed. "Could you ask for a better implement than a spike?" Almost in the same breath, she asked, "Aren't you curious about this too?" She showed them the letter and then turned her attention to the brass chest.

Holding it firmly between her knees, she inserted a row of the spikes of one shoe under the edge of the lid, then used the other shoe as a hammer.

As she paused for a moment, Nancy remarked, "The lid on this mystery chest is stubborn."

Bess said, "Why don't you stop for a while? It's almost dinnertime. We should dress."

Reluctantly Nancy agreed.

The girls had just finished changing when a boy appeared at the door bearing two boxes from the florist shop.

"They're for Nancy, of course." Bess sighed wistfully. "Barty is a pest but at least he's generous."

George looked at one of the boxes. "This is addressed to me!" she cried in surprise. "There must be some mistake."

Nancy thoroughly enjoyed herself as she watched the two girls open their boxes. So far they did not suspect that she had sent the flowers.

"Oh, what a lovely bouquet!" Bess exclaimed in delight, putting her face close to the yellow roses in it. "Who could have sent it?"

George was peering at the attached card. " 'From A Friend,' " she read.

"And mine is the same," Bess added.

"Are you sure you haven't been hiding something from me?" Nancy asked teasingly.

The little game went on for some time. Then Nancy's broad smile betrayed her.

"Nancy Drew, you sent these flowers!" Bess suddenly accused her.

"Well, yes, I did."

"It was great of you to do this, Nancy," Bess declared.

George thanked her, saying it was a "sweet" joke—the kind she liked.

"I did myself a good turn by visiting the florist.

"The lid on this mystery chest is stubborn,"
Nancy remarked

I found out something interesting about Barty."

Nancy explained that the girl in the flower shop had written the note which accompanied her roses.

"Barty seems to be afraid someone will recognize his handwriting," Bess remarked. "Do you suppose he's a fugitive?"

"He seems to have plenty of money and apparently doesn't work," Nancy replied. "Still, it never occurred to me that he might be a criminal."

"Why don't you wear one of Barty's flowers, Nancy?" Bess suggested. "It would set off your dress beautifully."

"But I don't like him," Nancy protested.

"Oh, probably he won't even be in the dining room. Flowers are flowers, Nancy. Here, let me pin a rose on you," George insisted.

Nancy finally gave in. She hid the chest under the bed, and the girls left their rooms, each wearing a rose.

Since Mr. Drew had not returned to the hotel the girls planned to eat alone. They were led by the headwaiter to a pleasant table near a window.

"Oh, there's Barty," Nancy murmured to George as she noticed him seated alone at a table nearby. "Don't let on you see him."

It was impossible to avoid the man, however, because he immediately got up and came over to them. When he saw that Nancy was wearing one of his roses, the glance he bestowed on her was more than just friendly.

"May I join you?" he asked. Then, without waiting for a reply, he seated himself in the empty chair beside Nancy.

During dinner Bartescue enjoyed himself thoroughly. He idled over his food as he recounted his fantastic adventures in Africa. Nancy suspected that he had never been there.

Finally the meal came to an end. With feelings of relief the girls left the dining room. Bartescue followed.

"Of course you're staying downstairs for the dancing," he said to Nancy.

"No, I must see the doctor. He's going to examine my hand again and give his verdict on whether or not I can play in the tournament."

"You are very courageous. Few players would attempt it with such an injury."

Nancy made no comment. She gave a polite smile of farewell and moved away.

As Dr. Aikerman examined her injured hand, the three girls waited in anxious silence. He asked Nancy a question or two regarding the pain.

"Only one finger is stiff now," she replied. "Please say I can play."

CHAPTER VI

The Caddy's Clue

"WELL, young lady," Dr. Aikerman said to Nancy, "I see you've set your heart on playing."

"Yes."

"Okay. I'll permit you to play on one condition. You must not remove this bandage."

Nancy frowned slightly. How could she hope to make a low score with one hand bandaged?

"I agree," she replied reluctantly.

"And another thing," the doctor added. "If your hand begins paining after you've started to play, you must default the match. Otherwise I won't be responsible for your case."

"I promise," Nancy murmured.

The girls were rather subdued as they went to their rooms.

"I don't think you should try to play in the tournament," Bess declared. "If you don't participate, people will realize it's because of your injured hand. It's no disgrace to default."

"But I want to play," Nancy replied. "My mind is made up."

"Then," George said, "if you're determined to do it, the best thing is to go to bed and get all the rest you can."

"I have work to do before I go to sleep," Nancy announced. With a nod she indicated the carved brass chest under the bed.

"Let Bess and me try to open it," George urged. "Here, give me that spiked shoe, Nancy. You're apt to hurt your hand again."

Eagerly the cousins took turns prying at the stubborn lid of the mysterious chest.

Finally Bess exclaimed, "It's loosening! Yes, it's coming! Nancy, you shall have the honor of opening the chest."

"It may be filled with worthless things." Nancy laughed, but her hand trembled with excitement as she slowly raised the lid.

The girls stared into the interior, their eyes fastened in awe on the amazing contents. Nancy was the first to recover from her astonishment.

"It's almost unbelievable!" she murmured in a half-whisper. "I never dreamed that the chest contained anything like this!"

The carved brass case was filled to the top with jewelry. Even a casual glance assured Nancy and her friends that the pieces were genuine. There were necklaces of rubies, emeralds and turquoise, also rings with unusual settings and many other gold and silver pieces.

"All this must be worth a fortune," Bess murmured. "Nancy, you'll be rich!"

"The jewelry isn't mine just because I found it."

"But the owner may never be located," George said hopefully as she lifted a silver bracelet from the chest. "Isn't this gorgeous?"

Nancy was attracted by an emerald necklace, but as she started to lift it from the chest she saw an object beneath it which was of far greater interest to her. The article was a jeweled compact!

Eagerly she picked up the gleaming container and opened it. A tiny picture was fitted into the lower half of the mirror! As Nancy showed it to her friends, Bess declared, "It's the photo of a child."

"Evidently it was ruined by water," George observed. "This looks like the picture of a little girl."

George and Bess could not imagine why Nancy should consider the discovery so important. She was tempted to tell them of her father's search for the possessor of just such an article. But recalling that the secret was not hers to reveal, she remained silent.

"Nancy, you don't seem pleased over all this treasure," Bess remarked as she and George continued to examine the beautiful pieces.

"I was just thinking—" Nancy answered absently. "I must show Dad the chest as soon as he returns to the hotel."

Shortly after eleven o'clock the girls heard Mr. Drew enter his room directly across the hall. Nancy lost no time in showing her father the carved brass chest. She threw open the lid, enjoying his look of amazement as he beheld the dazzling display of gems.

"Nancy, have you robbed a jewelry store?" he teased.

His daughter laughed and explained briefly how the chest had come into her possession. She climaxed the startling story by thrusting the jeweled compact into his hand.

"Dad, could this be the article we've been trying to trace?"

Carson Drew carefully examined the gleaming object.

"It certainly fits the description. And there's no question about the quality of the jewelry."

"Dad, the chest may have been hidden by a member of the gang of thieves."

"Yes, that's very possible. This discovery may change all our plans."

"And to complicate them, it will be harder to

track down the mysterious woman since she won't be carrying the telltale compact."

Carson Drew gave a sigh and suppressed a yawn. He said, "If this compact belongs to her—yes. We have no other clue. Suppose I keep this jewelry in my possession until I communicate with New York City detectives. I'll telephone immediately and give a description of every piece in the chest. Possibly they can identify the jewelry as stolen property."

Before saying good night, Nancy told her father that she was scheduled to play in the first round of the golf tournament the following day. Then she kissed him and went off to bed.

Nine o'clock the next morning Nancy was waiting at the first tee for Miss Amy Gray, whose name had been drawn with her own for the initial match.

Bess and George were on hand to see their friend's first drive. They had decided against following her over the course, fearing that their presence might prove distracting. Nancy had arranged for Chris to caddy for her. He smiled encouragingly as she took a few practice swings.

"How does your hand feel?" George inquired.

"Oh, fine," Nancy answered.

Amy Gray, about thirty and slightly plump, soon arrived with her caddy. She drove a ball which sped two hundred yards straight down the fairway. Calmly Nancy stepped to the tee and sent her own ball within a few feet of that of her opponent.

Bess and George were delighted at the beautiful shot. From the first tee, they watched the pair play the hole and were almost certain that Nancy had won by a stroke.

"She's starting off pretty well even if her hand does bother her," Bess declared gleefully.

Amy Gray was an able player and did not waste strokes. She took the second hole and the third, leaving Nancy on the defensive. After that, it was a grim fight with first one player having the advantage, then the other. Finally when Amy shot a ball into the river on the fifteenth fairway Nancy knew that she herself would win the match.

"You're playing a beautiful game," Amy congratulated her.

"I'm afraid my final score won't be as low as I'd like," Nancy replied. "That is, not unless I make pars on the last three holes. Number sixteen isn't my favorite, either."

She smiled significantly at Chris, who averted his eyes in embarrassment. He was still ashamed because he had refused to search for her lost ball near the haunted bridge.

Nancy sent a long ball flying down the fairway, and was glad it did not enter the woods. As she walked along with her caddy, she told him she had investigated the ravine.

"Your bridge has no ghost, Chris."

"But I've seen the—the thing moving about," the boy said defensively.

"What you saw through the trees was a white scarecrow."

"A scarecrow?" He laughed. "Well, that's a good joke on me and the other guys. We were sure it was a ghost because we could hear the thing screaming. How do you explain that?"

"I can't yet, Chris," said Nancy, "But I'm sure that the screams are not supernatural."

The boy looked doubtful. "I'm sorry I wouldn't look for your lost ball the other day," he apologized. "If I were sure you're right about the ghost I'd search for it later."

Nancy smiled in amusement because she saw that Chris was torn by conflicting emotions. He wanted to find the golf ball, but he could not rid himself of the fear he felt about looking for it.

Nancy said, "I'd especially like to recover that ball because it was autographed by Jimmy Harlow."

"Wow, no wonder you want to get it back," Chris murmured enviously. "I'll look for it."

"Have you always lived near Deer Mountain Hotel?" Nancy asked him as they were walking together toward the last hole.

"Sure." Chris grinned. "All my life."

"Then you must know nearly everyone for miles around. Tell me, did you ever hear of a house near the hotel that burned recently?"

The caddy looked slightly puzzled a moment, then he smiled.

"Oh, you must mean the Judson mansion. It stood over there."

With a sweep of his arm, Chris pointed back toward the woods. He said, "It was kind of close to the bridge—on the other side of the ravine. It burned more than two years ago in the middle of the night. No one knew how the fire started."

"You say a family named Judson lived in the house?"

"Not a family. Only Miss Margaret Judson."

"And is she an old lady?" Nancy inquired.

"Oh, no, she'd be about twenty-three or four now. Her parents died, and she was engaged to marry some guy—a professor at a college near here. But they never did get married. After the fire she ran away and no one heard much about her after that."

"It was odd that she disappeared directly after the fire," Nancy remarked.

"Yes, but the Judsons were strange. My mother could tell you a lot more about the family."

Nancy was elated. This was the first tangible clue she had had to the identity of the young woman with whom she had talked at Hemlock Hall. Would Chris's mother be able to tell her more regarding Margaret Judson—facts perhaps which would connect her with the brass chest discovered near her former home?

"Where do you and your mother live?" Nancy asked the caddy.

Chris gave his address and Nancy wrote it down. "I'll go to see her," she said.

CHAPTER VII

Ravine Riddle

NANCY played brilliantly on the eighteenth hole. Her hand had not pained her. Fortunately the bandage had not hampered the young golfer in driving the ball or using the putter to tap it into the cup.

Bess and George were waiting at the eighteenth green when Nancy and her opponent ended the round. They approached their friend the instant Amy Gray was out of hearing, and congratulated Nancy on winning the match.

"We knew you'd do it," Bess declared proudly. "Tomorrow you'll take the second round, and then you'll be well on your way to the championship!"

"It won't be easy," Nancy replied. "The second match is always harder than the first, because you're facing a better player."

"How was your score?" George asked.

"Not very good. I came in with an eighty. I must get down into the low seventies or under to win."

"You can do it, Nancy," Bess said confidently. "How about lunch, girls?"

"Great," Nancy agreed. "If we have it early maybe we won't run into Barty."

The three girls were relieved to find the hotel dining room practically deserted. After enjoying a leisurely meal they wandered out-of-doors. Nancy's gaze roved toward the sixteenth fairway.

"You're not considering more golf?" George asked in surprise.

Nancy shook her head. "Eighteen holes is enough for me today. Chris was telling me about an old mansion which burned a couple of years ago. Miss Margaret Judson, the owner, lived there. The place is over in the general direction of the bridge. Let's hike to it." She chuckled. "Maybe we'll find another lost treasure."

Though the idea of the trek did not appeal to Bess, she and George agreed to accompany Nancy. The three were cutting across the fairway of the eighteenth hole when they encountered Bartescue.

"Hello," he called. "Where are you going?"

"Oh, on a little hike," Nancy replied as he fell into step with them.

He said quickly, "I have a little time to kill before I play my match this afternoon."

"I doubt if we'll be back very soon," Nancy

said pointedly. "You might miss your match if you come along."

"In other words, 'no gentlemen wanted.' " Bartescue laughed. "Oh, well, I was only teasing. I couldn't have gone anyway because I tee off at one-thirty." With a wide, knowing grin he left.

"Do you think Barty suspects we're on a special search?" Bess asked in an undertone a moment later.

"He acted as if he does," Nancy said.

Glancing over their shoulders to make certain they were not being watched, the girls cut through the woods. They approached the old wooden bridge cautiously.

"The scarecrow is waving its arms back and forth as usual," Bess observed nervously as they glimpsed it through the trees. "I have a strong hunch that we're walking straight into trouble."

George laughed at Bess's fears. "Don't be negative," George said.

Nancy looked up and down the stream. "This is probably the only place near here to cross the ravine," she said. "I think the bridge should bear our weight if we walk over one at a time."

The young detective went first. After she safely reached the opposite side, George followed. Bess came last, uttering a muffled little shriek as the flapping scarecrow brushed her arm.

"Sh—sh!" Nancy warned. "We don't want to broadcast our arrival."

"You'd scream too if that thing wrapped itself around—" Bess retorted.

George interrupted. "Nancy, I don't see how you expect to find the burned mansion when you don't know the way." She ducked to avoid being scratched by a low-hanging thorny branch. "Did Chris say it was on this side of the bridge?"

Nancy replied, "He pointed toward the left in this general direction. I think we're heading right. I see a trail."

Nancy indicated a faintly outlined path directly ahead. When the girls reached it they were puzzled to find still another trail branching away from the ravine.

"Which shall we take?" Bess asked as Nancy hesitated. "It looks as if the one that follows along the edge of the ravine might have been used recently."

"Yes, so probably it's the other one. Anyway, let's try it," Nancy suggested.

She pushed forward again, the scraggly bushes tearing at her clothing. Bess and George followed as best they could. Presently the trio came to a clearing enclosed by a high, uncut hedge.

"Thank goodness we're out of that jungle at last." Bess sighed wearily as she leaned against a tree to rest. "Do you suppose this is the estate, Nancy?"

The young detective craned her neck. "Yes, I can see something directly ahead that looks like part of a building. This must have been a beautiful place when it was kept up."

The grounds covered about five acres, and were wooded with giant oak and willow trees. What probably had been a lush green lawn was choked with weeds, but the vestiges of a rose garden remained.

There was a huge pile of debris in the very center of the clearing. A charred pillar and several half-burned timbers rose from it. Little else remained of the pretentious mansion.

"Is this what we've come to see?" Bess asked in disgust.

"What did you expect—that some genie had restored the house?" George replied.

Nancy said nothing. It had not occurred to her that the Judson fire had been so devastating. She had hoped the charred remains would yield a clue, such as a photograph, to connect some member of the family with the mysterious brass chest. Observing Nancy's look of disappointment, her friends shrewdly guessed that she had not told them everything.

"Do you know anything more about Miss Judson?" Bess asked curiously.

"Chris told me she's a young woman who has had a tragic life."

"I don't see how you hope to connect her with the brass chest," George remarked.

Nancy smiled. "I'm afraid I can't tell you anything more until Dad gives me permission. I can see there's nothing to find here, so let's start back to the hotel."

Bess and George did not urge their friend to reveal her secret because of her promise to her father. Few words were exchanged as the three friends made their way laboriously back to the ravine.

Nancy was absorbed with her own thoughts. Could Margaret Judson be a member of the international gang of jewel thieves?

"No, not if I'm any judge of character. She just didn't look like the type," Nancy reflected.

Her thoughts were interrupted as a shrill scream broke the stillness. The three girls stopped abruptly.

"There it is again!" Bess murmured apprehensively, clutching Nancy's hand. "That awful scream!"

The girls waited a moment, listening, but the noise was not repeated.

"I'd certainly like to find out who or what is making that sound," said Nancy.

"I'm not sure I would," said George.

"It's all part of the ravine mystery," Nancy remarked, "but how does it figure in?"

The girls went on. Presently they reached the dividing point of the two trails. Nancy's gaze roved down the path along the ravine.

"I think the sound came from that direction," she said firmly. "Let's investigate—"

"Not me," Bess cried, grasping Nancy's arm. "I've had enough adventure for one day, thank you."

Nancy's protests were overruled, and she was fairly pulled along toward the haunted bridge. One at a time the girls crossed it and retraced their steps toward the golf course.

To keep out of the way of players who might be coming down the fairway, Nancy and her friends walked within the fringe of woods. Now and then they could hear voices and knew that a match was being played somewhere nearby.

Suddenly an object came whizzing through the air, striking a tree not more than a dozen yards from where the girls were walking. It was a golf ball and landed squarely behind another tree.

"Someone will have a mean shot to play," Nancy remarked. "Let's duck out of sight and watch."

The girls had just hidden behind some trees when Martin Bartescue entered the woods. He was muttering to himself, savagely berating "his luck." The man hunted among the shrubbery for a few minutes and finally came upon his ball.

"Never mind, caddy," the girls heard him shout. "I've found it."

Satisfied that no one was watching, he took an

iron club and deftly raked the ball from the hollow spot in which it had lodged. Now, with it lying in an unobstructed path to the fairway, he played a clean shot out of the woods.

"Did you see that?" Nancy whispered in great disgust. "He cheated!"

CHAPTER VIII

The Gardener's Scare

"SOMEONE should report Barty to the golf committee," Bess declared angrily. "The nerve of him to move his ball!"

"He ought to be barred from further competition," George added.

"I agree," Nancy said.

When the girls reached the hotel they found Carson Drew seated on the terrace. After he had chatted with the three for a few minutes he took Nancy aside and told her that he would have to leave immediately to catch a plane to New York.

"I'd appreciate your driving me to the airport and keeping my car. I must go because New York detectives have asked me to bring the brass chest and its contents there for examination," he explained.

"Then they think the jewelry may be stolen property?" Nancy asked quickly.

"Yes. Nancy, keep your eyes open for that woman you encountered at Hemlock Hall. She'll probably be wanted for questioning."

"All right, Dad. I suspect that her name may be Margaret Judson but I have no proof."

"You've done remarkable work on the case so far," Mr. Drew praised his daughter warmly. "While I'm gone, watch out. Remember that the woman we're after is shrewd and dangerous."

"I'll be careful."

In the morning Nancy learned that her golf match would not be played until later in the day.

"Girls," she said to Bess and George, "I'm driving down to the village to call on Chris's mother. He said she could tell me more about the Judsons and their burned home."

Chris had told his mother to expect Nancy. Mrs. Sutter greeted her cordially. She proved to be a loquacious woman who launched into a long account of her children's achievements and talents. With difficulty Nancy managed to change the subject and talk about the Judson family.

"Oh, yes," Mrs. Sutter said with a nod. "Chris was telling me you were interested in them, though I told him I didn't see why anyone would be. They were aloof people, never mixing with their neighbors.

"Margaret was pretty but she aged a lot after her parents died. She was engaged to marry a college professor. I don't know what happened. After the fire, she just ran off. I did housework for a woman who knew the young man. She told me he was all broken up over it and has not married."

"Why did Margaret run away?"

"Some said it was because she was so upset over her parents' death, and then the fire on top of it. Others thought maybe she just wanted to break the engagement and didn't have the courage to tell the professor."

"Isn't any member of the Judson family living in the community now?"

"Oh, no. They're all gone and no one knows what became of Margaret Judson except perhaps the gardener."

Mrs. Sutter did not recall the man's name nor where he lived.

"I heard that he goes to the Judson place sometimes and cuts the weeds. But I guess he's given up hope that Margaret will ever return."

"Have you any idea how I can find this gardener, Mrs. Sutter?"

"Not unless you happen to run into him by accident. He doesn't come to town very often and I don't know anyone who could tell you where he lives."

"I'd really like to find him," Nancy murmured.

"You're pretty interested in the family, aren't you?" Mrs. Sutter asked.

Nancy could see that Mrs. Sutter was overcome

with curiosity. "I found something near the golf course which I thought might belong to Margaret Judson. That's why I'm trying to trace her."

The explanation partially satisfied Mrs. Sutter, and Nancy left before the woman could ask any more questions. On her way to Deer Mountain Hotel she stopped her car at a service station to get gas. She learned from the attendant that the Judson estate could be reached by a dirt road which ran south of the ravine.

"I'll drive out there on the chance the gardener may be cutting weeds," Nancy decided. "I'll still have time to get back for my golf match."

The trip to the Judson estate took a little over half an hour. Nancy left the car by the roadside and walked up an overgrown lane to the estate. At first she thought the place was deserted. Then suddenly she glimpsed a man some distance away. He was cutting weeds with a hand sickle.

As Nancy moved forward eagerly, he looked up. Seeing her, he dropped his sickle and started to run in the opposite direction.

"Wait!" Nancy begged him. "Please wait!"

The man paid no attention. He leaped onto a bicycle hidden in the bushes, then rode rapidly down a path and disappeared among the trees.

"Don't run away!" Nancy shouted as she dashed after him.

The man glanced over his shoulder and peddled faster and faster. Breathless from running, Nancy was compelled to abandon the chase. In chagrin she watched him vanish from view.

"Now why did he act that way?" she speculated, frowning.

With a shrug Nancy turned and walked back to her car. At the hotel Bess and George were waiting for her on the terrace.

"Barty won his match yesterday," Bess announced as Nancy sat down. "George and I happened to see the scorecard."

"What did he have on number sixteen?" Nancy asked quickly.

"A four. Imagine that!"

"He should have been disqualified for cheating," Nancy said. "Did you tell the chairman about it?"

"We were going to, but what was the use?" George asked. "He would deny everything."

"Yes, that's true," Bess added.

"Barty was ahead before he came to the sixteenth hole," George revealed. "He didn't need to cheat for the match already was his. He just couldn't bear to take a penalty."

"It's disgusting," Nancy murmured. "I wonder how the other matches are turning out. Let's watch some of the players."

They sauntered along the course, pausing at the seventeenth green to watch two players hole their putts. Then they moved on toward the woods.

"Isn't that Chris Sutter?" Nancy asked presently, indicating a boy just within the fringe of trees.

"He's peering into the woods at the identical place where your ball went in," Bess observed.

"I tried to convince him that the area wasn't haunted," Nancy said with a chuckle.

It was obvious that he was still afraid to look for the ball. Finally, mastering his misgivings, he disappeared from view. The girls quickened their steps.

Just as they reached the woods, Chris reappeared, apparently unsuccessful in his search for the golf ball.

"No luck?" Nancy asked him.

The boy shook his head. "Sorry."

"By the way, Chris," Nancy said, "I'm depending on you to caddy for me today."

"I'll be ready whenever you say, Miss Drew."

"Please be at the first tee by two-thirty. Our match will be a hard one."

"You'll win," Chris said confidently, "and I'll be pulling for you all the way."

The girls chatted with Chris for a few minutes. Then, leaving him to continue the search for the autographed golf ball, they walked back to the hotel for luncheon.

While passing through the lobby Nancy saw a letter in her room mailbox. She stopped to ask the clerk for it.

"I'll bet it's a note from your new admirer," Bess declared, giggling.

The letter was indeed from Martin Bartescue. He wished Nancy luck in her afternoon match, and said that he had defeated his opponent by an easy margin.

"If you win today, we must celebrate our joint victory," he had written. "I look forward to escorting you to the dance at Hemlock Hall."

"Hm!" Nancy fumed. "He takes it for granted that I'd be thrilled to go." Then, calming down, she added, "I think perhaps I'll accept."

Bess and George stared at her in bewilderment.

"How can you expect to have any fun with him?" George asked.

"I don't. But it'll be a good chance to study the guests—investigative work for Dad."

"Oh, that's different," Bess answered in relief. "By the way, two boys here at the hotel have asked George and me to the same dance."

"We haven't promised yet," Bess replied, "but if you want to go with Barty we could accept and all keep together."

"Good idea," Nancy agreed after a moment's thought. "And now, let's eat lunch. I'll have to leave soon for my match."

Later, when the girls came from the dining room, the desk clerk signaled to Nancy. He handed her a telegram that had just been delivered. It was from her father and read:

MEET ME AT AIRPORT TOMORROW MORNING
AT SEVEN. JEWELRY IN BRASS CHEST
EXAMINED. WE MUST LOCATE OWNER.

Immediately Nancy thought, "Maybe I'll have some news for Dad. There's a chance I may see Margaret Judson at Hemlock Hall tonight! For once perhaps Barty has done me a favor by inviting me to the dance there."

It was after two o'clock when the girls walked to the first tee. Nancy resolutely put aside all thoughts of the baffling mystery. Her opponent, a stout, muscular woman, nodded curtly as she tested out her swing.

Bess whispered to Nancy, "This isn't going to be a friendly match. Ruth Allison is out to win!"

The two players matched each other stroke for stroke as they played the first three holes. Neither seemed able to gain the advantage. Nancy was conscious that her opponent watched every shot like a hawk, as if hoping to catch Nancy breaking one of the rules of the game. Nancy in turn paid careful attention to every move she made.

Her hand pained her, but she made no mention of the handicap under which she was playing. At first Nancy was able to drive long, straight balls, but gradually her hand became weary and she found herself in difficulty.

Ruth Allison won two holes in succession. A look of smug satisfaction came over her face. It faded, however, when Nancy, fighting gamely, took the next hole, matched her opponent in the following one, and then won again to even the score.

At the sixteenth tee the match was still even. Having won the previous hole, Nancy had the honor of driving first. As she took a backswing with her club, her mind wandered momentarily to the mystery of the jewel thefts. The result was that her ball sliced wickedly. To the horror of Chris it entered the woods.

"Too bad," Ruth Allison said with a false show of sympathy. "I'm afraid that will put you out of the tournament."

CHAPTER IX

Nancy Is Accused

RUTH ALLISON's remark that Nancy's bad drive might put her out of the tournament upset the teen-age girl. She tried not to show it. Nancy watched in dismay as her opponent drove a long, straight ball past the spot where hers had gone into the woods. The group walked along in silence.

"Cheer up, Nancy," said Bess. "There are still two holes to play. You could win yet."

Chris summoned up his courage and plunged into the woods. He located Nancy's ball in a hollow spot by a tree.

"It's almost unplayable," he told her when she caught up to him. Ruth Allison had walked on, a self-satisfied expression on her face.

Nancy asked Chris for her mashie and struck the ball with all her strength. The shot was remarkable. The ball flew up and sailed cleanly out of the woods.

"Marvelous!" George called out.

Despite Nancy's remarkable play, her score was one point higher than her opponent at the end of the hole.

As they walked to the next tee, Nancy remarked, "I'm one down now, and—" She started to add that her hand was paining her but quickly broke off.

Nancy had no intention of giving up easily, and managed to tie Ruth Allison on the seventeenth. As they played toward the last green, she put all her strength into each shot, wincing with pain every time.

"A tie isn't enough here," she said to herself grimly. "I must win by a stroke or I'll lose the match and be out of the tournament!"

A small crowd had gathered by the green to watch the players come in. Ruth Allison, with victory so near, became excited and made a wild putt. Nancy dropped her ball into the cup, tying the match again.

According to the rules, the players had to keep on until one or the other had a lower score. Nancy wondered how much longer her hand could endure the strain.

As the two players went back to the first tee the crowd followed. An audience seemed to bother Ruth Allison. Her drive was short, and her next shot went into the rough. She lost the hole by two strokes. It was Nancy's match!

"Oh, you were great!" Bess praised her friend gleefully, while George hugged her.

Ruth Allison, instead of offering congratulations, turned on her heel and stalked angrily toward the golf clubhouse office.

"What a poor sport she turned out to be!" George said in disgust.

When the applause of the crowd was over, Nancy and her friends walked away slowly. They noticed a man who was on the tournament committee hurrying toward them. It was evident from the expression on his face that something was amiss.

"Miss Drew, will you come with me, please?" he requested her quietly. "There seems to be a little misunderstanding. Your opponent claims the match."

"Why? I won it fairly," Nancy replied as she followed the man. "There were witnesses."

"Miss Allison claims the match on account of the sixteenth hole," the man told her gravely. "She says that you moved your ball after it went into the woods."

Nancy was stunned by the false accusation. In the office she faced Miss Allison and demanded, "How can you say such a thing? You know it isn't true."

"It certainly is," the woman retorted. "I'm sure

you moved your ball. Otherwise you never could have reached the fairway in one shot. I distinctly heard your caddy tell you that the shot was unplayable."

"Nevertheless, I made it."

Bess and George had followed their friend to the golf office. Unable to remain quiet, they flew to her defense.

"Nancy has never cheated in her life!" George burst out angrily. "You're just mad because she beat you!"

"Now, let's be calm about this," the tournament chairman said anxiously. "We'll try to decide this matter fairly—"

"What's the trouble?" asked a masculine voice behind them.

The girls turned. Martin Bartescue was standing in the doorway. He repeated his question and the tournament chairman reluctantly explained the difficulty.

"Why, Miss Allison's accusation is utterly false," he stated firmly. "It so happens that I was walking along the woods as the match was being played. I saw Miss Drew drive into the trees, and I watched her execute her shot onto the fairway. It was a beauty."

"Oh, thank you," Nancy gasped gratefully. For the first time she decided that Barty had his good points.

"If everyone defends Miss Drew I may as well

drop the charge!" Ruth Allison said haughtily and left the office.

"Don't mind her," the tournament chairman said to Nancy. "She always loses hard. I'm sorry to have embarrassed you."

Bartescue followed the girls outside, smirking with pleasure.

"Did you really see me play my shot?" Nancy asked him.

"Why certainly," he returned, his eyes twinkling. "Didn't you see me?"

"No, I didn't."

"You must have been looking in another direction. By the way, did you get my note?"

"Yes," Nancy admitted and politely accepted his invitation to the dance at Hemlock Hall.

He said good-by and walked off. Nancy could not rid herself of the suspicion that Bartescue had lied about being in the woods. Later that afternoon, while the three girls were in the soda shop, they were amazed to have the boy at the counter mention Bartescue to them.

"He's a funny guy," the boy said. "Spent a long time in here earlier this afternoon. He wrote out a telegram, but crumpled it up. As a matter of fact, he wrote out two or three, but couldn't seem to get one that suited him. He left one wadded up on the counter and I read it."

"You did?" Nancy said.

"Sure, see, here it is." The boy took a crumpled

"Nancy has never cheated in her life!"
George burst out

paper from his pocket and waved it. Nancy was able to make out two words in the quick glance she got of the message—Margaret Judson.

"Want to read it?" the boy asked.

Nancy shook her head. "No, I'm not interested in Mr. Bartescue's private affairs."

The boy thrust the paper into his pocket again and a moment later was called away to wait on another customer. Nancy left the shop with Bess and George.

She wondered if she had made a mistake in declining to read the telegram. What connection could Barty have with Margaret Judson?

"I caught only a glimpse of the writing," she said, "but I'm sure it wasn't the same as any of the other samples of Barty's." She paused, then continued, "About the dance tonight. I'd like you and your dates to follow us closely in your car."

"We'll do our best to keep you in sight," Bess promised.

"I hope I won't need to send out an SOS." Nancy laughed.

Shortly before nine o'clock the boys who were to escort Bess and George arrived in their car. Nancy was worried that Barty would ruin her plans by being late, but to her relief he appeared within a few minutes.

As he assisted her into his car, Nancy glimpsed her friends in a nearby convertible, waiting to follow. For a time her escort drove at a moderate pace. When the road straightened out he speeded up until the other car was left far behind.

"Oh, let's not go so fast!" Nancy protested.

"This is the way I like to travel," Barty told her.

"Well, I don't. If you refuse to slow down, I'll never go out with you again."

"All right," he grumbled, and grudgingly reduced the speed of the car.

For some minutes they rode in silence. Nancy was wondering how to broach the subject of Miss Allison's accusation about cheating. Finally, with a pretense of being facetious, she suggested that perhaps he had not really seen her hit the ball out of the woods.

"You were just coming to my defense, weren't you?"

"I guess maybe you're right," Barty admitted. "Did you cheat?"

"Certainly not!"

"It wouldn't make any difference to me if you had or hadn't," Barty replied.

Nancy was not flattered. She wanted to tell him how important and enjoyable it was to play any competitive game honestly and with a good sportsmanlike attitude. But she decided she would gain nothing by revealing her true feelings. Taking a different tack, she cajoled her escort into a pleasant mood and casually asked him if he knew Miss Judson whose house had burned.

"Margaret Judson?" he inquired indifferently. "Oh, I met her in Europe three years ago. A pretty woman, but boring."

"Where is she living now?"

"She doesn't wish to have her address revealed."

"I thought she might be staying near here," Nancy said, watching him closely.

"Perhaps she is." Bartescue smiled.

Another silence followed, which was not broken until they reached Hemlock Hall. Nancy excused herself to go to the powder room. She stayed there hoping to see Margaret Judson among the persons who came and went. Bess and George arrived and she left the room with them.

"Try not to lose Barty's car going back to the hotel," Nancy urged. "In the meantime keep your eyes open for a woman with a jeweled compact. If you see one, please report to me instantly."

"Will do," Bess promised.

The music was excellent, but Nancy did not enjoy dancing with Bartescue. Finally she went to the ladies' lounge. There she maintained an alert watch for a woman with a jeweled compact.

"This night will be entirely wasted," she thought in disappointment. "Miss Judson isn't here and there's not a single clue to help Dad's case."

Reluctantly Nancy returned to dance with her date. When the music stopped, he took her to a chair and excused himself. "I'll be back in a few minutes," he said, and went off.

Nancy got up and wandered into a small room adjoining the ballroom to get some fresh air. The place was vacant. Nancy turned to leave but halted when she heard a low murmur of voices.

Two women seated on the porch outside were conversing earnestly near an open window. Their words reached Nancy clearly.

"But I tell you I have no money to give you for the compact," the one said in a harassed tone. "Please try to understand."

"How do I know you didn't sell it?" the other asked harshly.

The women lowered their voices so Nancy was unable to hear anything. She moved swiftly toward the window to listen.

"I must learn who they are," Nancy thought excitedly. "One of those women may be Margaret Judson!"

CHAPTER X

Telltale Photograph

APPARENTLY the two women on the porch heard someone coming. They arose and moved away, walking hurriedly toward the garden.

By the time Nancy came outdoors, they were too far away for her to distinguish either woman in the darkness. But the young detective observed that one was dressed in a flowered silk gown which hung in long, loose folds from her shoulders.

"Could she be Margaret Judson?" Nancy asked herself.

In a few moments they had vanished. Nancy ran down the steps into the garden, sure that the women had taken one of the winding paths leading from the hotel.

"I must find them!" she thought.

A number of couples were enjoying the moonlight, some idling near the fountains. Others were walking slowly up and down as they listened to strains of music from the dance orchestra. Nancy darted here and there, searching frantically.

Suddenly, far ahead of her, she thought she saw the woman in the flowered silk dress. Nancy rushed forward. Just then a young couple came from among the trees. Nancy, unable to stop, ran full tilt into them.

"Oh, I'm terribly sorry," she apologized. "You're not hurt, are you?"

"No," the man replied, "but watch your step."

Nancy took another path, this time more slowly. But she could not find the woman in the flowered silk and her companion. Finally Nancy gave up and went back to the hotel lobby. One of the women she sought was just entering an elevator!

"Now's my chance!" Nancy decided.

She was too late to catch the elevator but raced upstairs. Nancy reached the next floor just as the elevator stopped there. The woman in the flowered dress alighted. But she was not Margaret Judson.

On a sudden hunch Nancy said to her, "Pardon me, but do you know where Miss Judson is?"

The woman gazed at the girl in surprise but replied, "Probably she has gone to her room."

Nancy was amazed to hear Miss Judson was registered at the hotel. The other day the young woman had said that she was not staying there. "Do you know the number of her room?"

"No."

Nancy hurried downstairs to ask the desk clerk. "She just left here," he reported. "Decided not to stay after all."

"Oh!" Nancy gasped. "Can you tell me her forwarding address?"

"She left none."

The young detective was mulling over this bit of news when Martin Bartescue sauntered up.

"Oh, here you are," he said with a trace of annoyance in his tone.

"I didn't mean to run off," Nancy replied quickly. "I thought I saw Miss Judson enter the elevator. I want to speak with her. Have you seen her tonight?"

He answered with a mysterious smile, "Let's forget Miss Judson and enjoy this next dance."

Against her will Nancy was led back to the ballroom. She did not try to escape from her partner again. Shortly before the last dance, she found an opportunity to remind Bess and George to follow closely in their car during the ride back to the hotel.

Despite Nancy's fears, the homeward drive proved to be uneventful. She tumbled into bed, tired and discouraged by her unsuccessful detective work that evening.

Nancy wondered if Barty had gone to the dance to meet Margaret Judson. The weary young sleuth fell asleep. At six she was awakened by the alarm on her travel clock.

"Who left that turned on?" Nancy moaned drowsily. Then she remembered having set it herself. Soon it would be time for her to drive to the airport to meet her father.

By seven o'clock father and daughter were seated opposite each other at a table in the airport restaurant.

"Did you have a successful trip, Dad?" his daughter asked as soon as they had given their breakfast order. "What did you learn about the contents of the brass chest?"

"The New York police said only one article in the entire collection proved to be stolen property."

"The jeweled compact?"

"Yes. The other articles couldn't be identified. Of course, they may have been stolen recently and the theft was not reported. At any rate, the jewelry, with the exception of the compact, is not on the list of articles smuggled into this country by the international gang."

Nancy listened to a more detailed account of her father's visit to New York. Then she revealed her own recent activities.

"I was sure I'd located Miss Judson at Hemlock Hall," Nancy finished. "But she got away before I could talk to her."

"We must trace her," Mr. Drew said. "From the clues you've gathered I'm certain she's the woman we're after."

The lawyer wished to drive without delay to Hemlock Hall to look for Margaret Judson, and Nancy was glad to accompany him. The trip proved to be a waste of time. Although they inquired at the airport, gas stations and various shops, no one could give them any information about Miss Judson's whereabouts.

"Dad," said Nancy, "I'm afraid I'll have to stop sleuthing and hurry back to our hotel. My name is posted to play in the golf tournament at two o'clock."

The Drews ate lunch, then drove to Deer Mountain. Nancy quickly changed to golf clothes and went out on the course. As usual, Chris was her caddy.

The match was close. Nancy, scarcely noticing the pain in her hand, played an excellent game. To the delight of her friends, she won on the fifteenth hole. As she finished out the round, she jokingly asked Chris if he had found her Jimmy Harlow ball.

"I don't think I'll ever find it now," he told her gloomily. "Maybe someone else picked it up."

"Have you noticed anyone in the woods by the bridge?" Nancy asked.

"This morning I saw a man poking a stick around in the mud by the stream."

Nancy pressed for a more detailed description of the person, but Chris was unable to give one.

On her way back to the hotel she reflected on the clue that Chris unknowingly had revealed.

"That man he saw may have been the Judson gardener," she thought. "Or possibly someone who was searching for the brass chest I found buried in the mudbank."

Nancy was afraid it might be too late to locate the man, but she decided to investigate the haunted bridge area immediately. Bess and George were eager to assist in Nancy's search. The three girls set off across the golf course. They had gone only a few steps when Bess stopped.

"Here comes that pest Barty!" she exclaimed. "Now what'll we do?"

Thinking very quickly, Nancy greeted the newcomer with a warm smile.

"Oh, Mr. Bartescue, did my father see you this afternoon?"

"Why no," he answered in surprise, falling into the trap. "Did he wish to speak with me?"

"Well, he was looking for a tennis partner."

Martin Bartescue had boasted to Nancy that he excelled in several sports. Tennis and golf, however, he claimed were his favorites.

"I see Dad on the terrace!" Nancy cried and motioned for him to join the group.

"Dad, I've found a wonderful tennis partner for you," she declared as he came up.

The lawyer suspected that Nancy wished to rid

herself of Bartescue, and agreed to get his tennis shoes and racquet and meet the other man at the courts.

The girls made their way toward the haunted bridge. Dark clouds were moving swiftly over-head, and by the time they reached the woods a strong wind was blowing.

Soon they were within view of the old bridge. Bess shivered and kept close to her companions. Suddenly they were startled to hear the same moaning and groaning sounds which had per-plexed them on their first visit.

"Oh!" Bess squealed, clutching George's arm.

Nancy warned her to be quiet, and for several minutes the girls stood perfectly still, waiting for the sound to be repeated. There was only a rustle of leaves in the breeze.

"I believe the noise came from somewhere right around here," said Nancy. "Let's investigate. Maybe we'll find someone's in hiding, playing a joke."

The girls searched through the brush and trees near both ends of the bridge, but found no one. Then they explored the trail they had seen on their previous visit which led along the ravine. Footprints were clearly visible. Had someone used the path within the past twenty-four hours?

A moment later a shrill scream broke the still-ness. This time Nancy was certain that the cry had come from some distance up the ravine.

"Let's go!" she urged excitedly. "We'll solve the mystery of these strange sounds yet!"

She darted forward along the path, oblivious to the thorny bushes that tore at her hair and clothing. Suddenly Nancy halted and stared. In a small clearing ahead was a log cabin. Smoke was curling lazily from the chimney.

"I didn't know anyone lived here in the woods," Bess gasped in surprise.

Nancy was debating what to do, when the cabin door opened and a man carrying a rifle emerged.

"He's the same one who was working near the Judson property," Nancy whispered. "I'll bet he's the gardener. Let's see what he's up to with that rifle," she added.

The man shouldered his gun and struck off in the general direction of the Judson property.

"I'm sure he's only going hunting," George declared.

Cautiously the girls followed him. Suddenly Bess tripped over a mossy log. As she fell headlong on the trail, she gave a faint outcry. The man immediately paused and glanced back. The trio crouched low.

Apparently satisfied that the sound he had heard was made by some wild animal, the hunter slowly walked on again. Moments later the girls heard a loud explosion and saw a sudden flash of fire. They gasped in horror as the man uttered a sharp moan of pain.

"He's hurt!" Nancy cried and darted forward.

The victim was lying still on the ground when the girls reached his side. Nancy bent anxiously over him and was relieved to find him breathing. A slight trickle of blood oozed from a wound in his forehead.

The young detective glanced at the man's rifle which lay on the ground a short distance away.

"His gun must have gone off accidentally," Nancy surmised, then added, "We'd better not move him. Let's get a doctor at once."

"I'll run back to the hotel," George offered.

"You're not afraid to cross the haunted bridge alone?" Bess asked quietly.

George shook her head. "Of course not."

As she hurried out of sight, Nancy studied the darkening sky. "I hope the rain holds off, at least until the doctor gets here," she said.

But within a few minutes it began to rain. Nancy and Bess carried the wounded man to his three-room cabin and laid him gently on a bed in the rear room. Bess looked for a clean towel and put a cold compress on his head.

Puddles of water were forming on the floor beneath the open windows. Nancy hurriedly closed them. One of the sashes in the bedroom was stuck fast and she looked about the kitchen for a tool to loosen it.

When she opened a drawer of the high cupboard, Nancy came upon an assortment of papers.

Thinking she might find a letter to identify the unconscious man, Nancy swiftly examined them. Suddenly her hand encountered a faded photograph between two sheets of stiff cardboard.

The picture was of a beautiful young girl. Across the bottom in a bold scrawl were the words:

> *To my faithful friend*
> *Joe Haley*
> > *Margaret Judson*

Nancy thought of the man who lay motionless on the bed. Was he Joe Haley and was Joe Haley the Judson gardener?

"The girl in the photograph is the one I met in the powder room at Hemlock Hall!" she told herself. "I was right about her identity."

"Nancy, aren't you going to close that window?" Bess broke in on her friend's reflections. "The wind is blowing directly across the bed."

After putting the photograph back in the drawer, Nancy continued her search for a tool. Finally she found a hammer and using it gently lowered the sash. At the same moment a wild cry came from behind the cabin.

"What was that?" Bess called in terror.

CHAPTER XI

Telephone Disguise

DETERMINED to learn the cause of the weird scream, Nancy flung open the cabin door.

"Don't leave me here alone!" Bess pleaded.

Her words fell on deaf ears. The young detective had darted out into the rain. She moved swiftly toward the rear of the cabin, certain the cry had come from there.

Nancy glanced about quickly but could see no one in the well-tended flower and vegetable garden or in the greenhouse. A few feet beyond, among the trees, she caught sight of a gleaming metallic object and hurried toward it.

As she drew closer Nancy was surprised to find that the gleam came from the heavy wire netting of a roofed wild-animal cage. Nancy's amazement grew as she observed that in it was a young mountain lion. She wondered if it belonged to Joe

Haley. The animal stopped pacing to raise its head and give a blood-chilling howl.

"So you don't trust me?" said Nancy, grinning. "Anyway, you've solved the mystery of the terrible screams we've been hearing."

She turned and started toward the cabin. Midway across the clearing Nancy saw Bess in the doorway motioning frantically.

"Nancy! Come here quickly!" she called out.

Nancy reached her, thoroughly drenched from the rain and breathless from running.

"What is it, Bess?" she asked.

"He—he," she said, indicating the wounded man on the bed, "started mumbling. I thought it might be important."

"Could you make out any of the words?" Nancy asked.

"He murmured something about a 'Miss Margaret' a moment ago," Bess replied.

As Nancy seated herself at the bedside, Mr. Haley began to toss restlessly on his pillow. It was difficult to restrain him. Then for several minutes the patient lay perfectly still.

His eyelids fluttered open and he mumbled, "Please, Miss Margaret—don't stay away. I can't find it—I've tried, but I can't." Mr. Haley's words ended in an incoherent mumble.

"What do you suppose he's been trying to find?" Bess asked.

Nancy shook her head.

Just then Bess cried out, "What was that? I thought I heard voices in the woods."

Nancy opened the cabin door, glad to find the rain had stopped. She stared in astonishment as six persons emerged from among the trees. George and Dr. Aikerman were in the lead. Directly behind them were Carson Drew and Ned Nickerson. Then came Burt Eddleton, George's friend, and Dave Evans, who dated Bess.

"Hi!" said everyone.

Nancy immediately led Dr. Aikerman to the patient, whom he said he did not know. The physician asked her to remain while he made his examination, in case he wanted her to get something for him.

Presently Nancy asked, "Is Mr. Haley badly injured?"

"I don't think so," he replied, without looking up. "The bullet only grazed him."

Mr. Drew had joined Nancy. Together they watched quietly as the physician dressed the man's wound. When he was finished, Mr. Haley stirred and moaned.

"He's coming around now," said the doctor.

"Would it be advisable to transfer him to a hospital?" asked Mr. Drew.

"It's not necessary," replied the physician. "He's lost a little blood and, of course, he is feeling the shock of the accident. But if he remains quiet and has good care he should be all right before too long."

Regretfully Nancy realized that she would not be able to question Mr. Haley in his weakened condition.

"I'll give him a sedative," said the doctor, "and stop by to see him tomorrow."

While he finished taking care of the injured man, Nancy and her father went back to the outer room and reported to the others.

"Who will take care of Mr. Haley?" asked Bess.

"I'll remain," Nancy offered quickly.

"That would mean you couldn't finish the golf tournament," said George. "And you have an excellent chance to win. Why not have a nurse?"

"A man is really needed around here," Nancy commented, and told about the mountain lion penned nearby.

Bess gasped. "Is that what we heard?"

"Yes," Nancy replied.

Ned spoke up. "How about Burt and Dave and me staying?" he proposed. "We've all had first-aid and camping experience. We could look after everything."

"We'll be glad to do it," Dave added, and Burt nodded in agreement.

"That would be a wonderful solution to the problem," Nancy said in relief, "but it doesn't seem fair to you, after coming to Deer Mountain for a good time."

Ned shrugged. "It would cost us a lot to stay at the hotel," he said with a grin. "This place is good enough."

After some discussion it was finally decided that the three boys would remain at the cabin. Dr. Aikerman approved and gave careful instructions for the care of the patient.

"Mr. Haley may be slow in getting his strength back," said the doctor. "He's been neglecting himself, I think. See that he gets plenty of hearty food and lots of sleep."

"Don't worry. We'll look after him," said Ned.

"And don't forget the wild beast," Bess reminded the boys.

"What is one supposed to feed a young mountain lion?" Ned asked.

"We'll have some raw meat sent out when we get back to town," Mr. Drew promised, "as well as a few other necessities that you may need here."

Nancy took Ned aside so that the others could not hear what she was saying.

"There's something I wish you'd do for me, Ned," she said.

"Sure. What is it?"

"Please listen very carefully to anything Mr. Haley says—whether he's conscious or talking in his sleep."

Ned glanced at Nancy, but he refrained from asking for an explanation, even though he regarded the request as strange.

"I'll be glad to," he promised.

"I wish you'd take down every word in writing," Nancy added as she turned to leave the cabin. "The solution of a very complex mystery may be in your hands."

Ned smiled. "Bet I'll solve it for you." Then they said good night.

Dr. Aikerman had brought his own car, and went off alone. As the three girls rode with Mr. Drew to Deer Mountain Hotel, Nancy asked, "By the way, Dad, did you win your tennis match against Mr. Bartescue?"

"No, he defeated me two out of three sets," Mr. Drew admitted ruefully.

"Oh, I was certain you'd beat him, Dad. He must be a good player."

"Far better than I expected. We had a few close decisions as to whether balls were inside or outside the court, but I'm offering no alibis. A defeat now and then is good for anyone." Mr. Drew chuckled.

At the hotel the lawyer explained to Nancy that it was necessary for him to drive to the village. "I'll buy supplies for the boys. While I'm there I'll check out an important lead in connection with my case."

After her father had driven away, Nancy and the other girls inquired at the hotel desk for mail. There were letters for Bess and George from their parents. Nancy found a note and a small package waiting for her. She studied the handwriting on them curiously.

"Hurry up and open the box," Bess urged. "I can't imagine what it contains."

Nancy removed the wrapping. She held up a golf ball for her friends to see. The gift had come from Martin Bartescue. His name was autographed neatly across the face of the ball.

"The note must explain about it," Bess declared.

Nancy tore open the envelope and found a message from Barty.

I'm sending you this ball to replace the one you lost. Use it in the tournament tomorrow and win!

Nancy was amused. "I guess he thinks his autograph is just as important as Jimmy Harlow's!"

"Will you use the ball tomorrow?" Bess inquired mischievously.

Nancy shrugged. Then, after a moment's pause, she announced, "No, but I'll keep it as a specimen of Mr. Bartescue's handwriting."

"Why does he always use a different signature?" George asked. "His handwriting never seems to be the same twice."

"I have a theory that he may be a forger," Nancy said in an undertone.

"Then why not report him to the police?" George suggested.

"Not yet. By playing a waiting game we may learn far more than we would if we were to expose the man immediately."

In her imagination she could see him linked with the jewel thieves. His acquaintance with the mysterious Margaret Judson, as well as his suspicious trick of altering his signature, perhaps to avoid identification, made it easy to visualize him as one of the gang.

A few minutes later in her room, Nancy reflected soberly, "Through Barty I might be able to trace Margaret Judson. And I *must* find her." Impulsively she looked at her watch, then sprang from her chair. Slipping into a coat, she said, "I'm taking the bus to town. Tell you why later."

There was no time to explain to Bess and George what she meant to do. The bus for town would leave the hotel in less than five minutes!

Nancy was the last passenger aboard. When the bus pulled away, she wondered if she should have waited until she had consulted her father about her plan. At the village she alighted and entered a drugstore. After making a purchase, she stepped into a telephone booth.

Summoning her courage, she called Deer Mountain Hotel and asked to speak with Mr. Martin Bartescue.

"It will be just my luck for him to be out," she thought anxiously.

Half a minute later she heard the man's voice at the other end of the line.

"Hello, who is it?" he demanded, as Nancy, overcome by nervousness, remained silent.

"This—is—Miss Judson," Nancy stammered, trying to speak in a nasal tone.

"Your voice doesn't sound natural."

"I have a bad cold."

"What is it you wish, Miss Judson? You know it isn't a good idea to call me here."

"I must speak with you about a very important matter. Can you meet me tonight?"

Bartescue grumbled, "I suppose so. Where shall we meet?"

"The same place and time as before."

"What's the matter with 2 B X Gardenia?"

Nancy was puzzled by the question, and for a moment could think of nothing to say. She did not have the slightest idea as to what 2 B X Gardenia could mean. In sheer desperation she mumbled into the telephone, "Nothing but the weather," and hung up before the man could reply.

As Nancy walked to the bus stop, she felt excited but also scared. Had Martin Bartescue guessed who was calling? Was 2 B X Gardenia a code for a meeting place? And if so, where was it?

CHAPTER XII

Stranded!

THE telephone conversation had served Nancy's purpose—it convinced her that Margaret Judson and Martin Bartescue could be working together in some nefarious business.

"I must follow Barty," she said to herself, "and find out where he goes."

Nancy returned to the hotel and explained her plan to Bess and George. "I'll borrow Ned's car and trail Barty when he leaves for his appointment with Margaret Judson."

Ned had given Nancy his key in case she wanted to use his car. Fortunately it was parked near the hotel exit and was ready to be driven out at a moment's notice.

"How about coming along?" Nancy asked her friends.

"You couldn't leave us home," George replied.

The girls went to dinner. They were pleased

that Bartescue was in the dining room so they could keep an eye on him. Before Nancy, Bess, and George were half through dinner, Barty abruptly rose and left.

"No dessert tonight," Nancy said hurriedly to the waiter. "We must leave now."

The three girls reached the lobby in time to see Barty depart by the front door.

"He intends to keep an appointment, all right," Nancy declared in satisfaction. "We must move fast or he'll be out of sight!"

They ran to Ned's parked car and Nancy started it quickly. Barty's automobile had vanished down the road, but Nancy drove rapidly and soon came within view of it.

"He seems to be heading for the village," she remarked.

Apparently unaware that he was being followed, Bartescue drove into town and parked across the street from a movie theater. Nancy stopped nearly a half block away and watched him cross the street and enter the building.

"Do you suppose he expects to meet Miss Judson inside the theater?" Bess asked in disappointment.

"Wait here," Nancy said, sliding from behind the steering wheel.

She bought a ticket to the theater and went inside. Although the usher could not recall the man Nancy described, the young detective was sure that Bartescue had entered the theater. In the darkened area she was unable to distinguish faces.

Thinking that possibly Barty had gone to the lounge to keep his appointment, she went there. The room was empty.

Perplexed, Nancy returned to the lobby, and after standing there for several minutes finally decided to join her friends again. She left the theater and crossed the street.

Suddenly she halted, staring blankly at the place where she had parked Ned's car. Bess, George, and the automobile had vanished!

Nancy was dismayed for an instant. During her absence had harm come to her friends? After a little sober reflection, Nancy convinced herself that George and Bess had driven off somewhere deliberately.

"Barty very likely came out of the theater shortly after I went inside," she reasoned. "The girls may have decided to follow him."

Nancy was temporarily stranded in the village. A bus would not return to Deer Mountain Hotel for nearly an hour.

Half an hour elapsed, and still there was no sign of the missing car. Nancy glanced anxiously at her watch.

"George and Bess may not return for hours," she said to herself. "Fortunately the hotel bus will be coming soon."

As she made her way toward the bus stop Nancy

heard the screech of brakes. Then a car came to a sudden halt by the curb.

"Nancy!" called a voice.

She whirled to see Ned Nickerson, who had driven up in his car. He sprang out to open the door for her.

"Bess and George sent me after you," he explained. "They're back at the hotel."

"At the hotel?"

"They didn't mean to run off, but right after you left, Bartescue came out of the theater by a side door, so they followed him."

"Where did he go?" Nancy inquired.

"Right back to the hotel. I happened to be there when the girls arrived. Since I wanted to talk to you, they asked me to come for you."

"I'm afraid," Nancy said, "that he suspected he was being followed."

"No doubt."

"Ned, tell me about the man at the cabin."

"He seems about the same, Nancy, but he did talk a good deal. As you thought, his name is Joe Haley. His most startling words were these:

" 'Miss Margaret, I'm afraid the box was stolen —don't cry—why don't you marry Mark?' "

"Are you sure the name was Mark?" Nancy asked quickly. "Could it have been Martin?"

"It might have been. I admit I didn't hear what he said very clearly."

"Ned, I forgot to ask you about Barty. Since he

claims to be acquainted with so many well-known society people, he should be in the Social Register. Did you look to see if his name is listed?"

"I did. It wasn't there."

"Just as I suspected."

On the way to the hotel Nancy told Ned as much as she felt she should about the case which had brought her father to Deer Mountain Hotel. Other facts in her possession were confidential. Without Mr. Drew's permission, she could not divulge them.

When they reached the hotel, Nancy learned from the desk clerk that her father had returned. She said good night to Ned and hastened to Mr. Drew's room.

"Any luck on your lead, Dad?" she asked eagerly.

"No," he said. "It was a worthless tip as usual." He sighed. "To tell the truth, I think we've been on the wrong track."

"How do you mean?"

"I doubt that Margaret Judson had anything to do with the jewel smuggling. There's no real evidence to support our theory that the brass chest belongs to her."

"I don't think she's guilty either," said Nancy. "She seems too nice. Cheer up, Dad," she added. "We'll get to the bottom of the mystery."

"That's my girl!" said Mr. Drew. "You'll win out, I know."

Nancy smiled. "Speaking of winning, tomorrow I face a crucial test in golf. I'd better get to bed."

"How does your hand feel?" her father asked anxiously. "Did you see Dr. Aikerman?"

"Yes, he let me take off the bandage, but said I still must be very careful."

"It's a shame you have to play with an injury," Mr. Drew said sympathetically. "I'm banking on you to win, anyway!"

"Thanks, Dad." Nancy smiled as she kissed him and went off.

She dropped in on Bess and George for a moment. George was writing letters, while Bess, propped up with pillows, had been reading in bed.

"Is your book a good one?" Nancy inquired.

Bess made a face. "The title sounded great, but it turned out to be about medieval history. It's pretty heavy reading. Here, take a look!"

She tossed the book across the room, expecting that her friend would catch it. Nancy was glancing in another direction and did not see the object flying toward her. In seconds the heavy volume had struck her injured hand.

"Oh!" she exclaimed, trying to smother a cry of pain.

Bess leaped from bed and ran to Nancy's side. "Oh, your poor hand! I thought you were watching when I tossed the book. I'll never forgive myself."

"The hand feels better already," Nancy assured her friend. "Please don't worry."

"But your match tomorrow—"

"The pain will go away before then, I'm sure."

Somewhat reassured, Bess returned to bed. She had no idea that Nancy actually was suffering intense pain.

As Nancy prepared for bed, she prayed for a night of restful sleep before the eventful day to come. But the ache in her hand grew steadily worse. She nervously paced the floor.

Finally she dialed Dr. Aikerman's room and told him what had happened.

"Come to my office in ten minutes," the physician replied.

Nancy dressed and went there. Dr. Aikerman was waiting for her.

"What have you been doing to this hand?" he asked sternly. "I hope you're not planning to play in the golf tournament tomorrow."

"Oh, doctor! Please don't say I shouldn't."

"That is a matter for you to decide, young lady. Your injury will not prove permanent, but I can see that you must be in excruciating pain at times."

"I am," Nancy admitted ruefully. "I was hoping you could relieve it."

"There is very little I can do except put on another bandage. It will take time for the hand to heal."

"The pain is so acute I haven't been able to sleep."

"I can give you something for that," the doctor said. "Perhaps by morning the pain will have lessened considerably."

Nancy thanked the doctor, and when she was back in her room took the medicine as directed. Soon she fell asleep and did not awaken until the sun streamed in through the window the following morning. As she opened her eyes Nancy heard someone rapping on the door connecting her room with that of Bess and George.

"May we come in?" Bess called.

"Yes," Nancy called back.

George opened the door and commented in surprise, "Not dressed yet?" Then, as she noticed how tired and wan her friend appeared, she added quickly, "Nancy, you've had a bad night!"

"I slept fairly well after the doctor gave me some medicine and bound my hand again."

"The doctor!" Bess exclaimed in dismay.

"Now don't start worrying," Nancy said. "My hand hurts only a little this morning, and I intend to play in the golf tournament."

She refused to say anything more about her injury, and started to dress. George and Bess tried in every way to assist her so she would not need to use her sore hand.

"You'll just have enough time to eat breakfast and reach the first tee," George said, glancing at her watch. "It's rather late."

The girls hastened to the dining room. They had just seated themselves when Nancy glimpsed Chris Sutter coming timidly toward her.

"Excuse me for bothering you, Miss Drew, but I want to talk to you about Miss Judson. My mother is here in the lobby and she has something to tell you."

Nancy arose quickly.

"Don't wait breakfast for me," she told Bess and George. "I'll go with Chris. This may be important!"

CHAPTER XIII

Unexpected Plunge

"HAVE you learned something about Margaret Judson?" Nancy inquired as she led Mrs. Sutter to a secluded corner in the hotel lobby. "Do you know where she's living now?"

"No, Miss Drew. That's what I want to talk with you about."

Nancy looked puzzled, and Mrs. Sutter hastened to explain. She had learned from the village postmistress that several letters addressed to Margaret Judson were being held for lack of a forwarding address.

"I thought you might have found out where she lives," the woman added.

"No, I haven't," Nancy answered.

It was clear to her now that Mrs. Sutter had come, not just to impart information, but to learn why Nancy was interested in Margaret Judson. The young detective cleverly avoided Mrs. Sutter's questions, but could not help feeling provoked because so much time had been wasted. She ended the conversation by explaining that her friends were waiting for her at the breakfast table.

Bess and George had just finished their meal. Since it was so late, Nancy ordered only orange juice and breakfast rolls.

"You can't win a golf tournament on a diet like that," protested Bess, who loved to eat.

"I must hurry. I was with Mrs. Sutter longer than I expected and learned nothing except that Margaret Judson hasn't picked up her mail for a long while."

The girls hastened to the hotel's golf office. They found the tournament chairman talking earnestly with a group of players who were to compete in the day's finals.

Betsy Howard, Nancy's opponent, explained to her, "There seems to be some mix-up. Our match has been postponed until one o'clock."

"I'm glad," said Nancy. "I really prefer to play this afternoon." Actually the young detective was delighted; she could do some more sleuthing.

Bess and George suggested that their friend rest in her hotel room while they played tennis, but Nancy told them she had other plans. After they had gone, she drove to the village to interview the postmistress. The woman consented to show her the letters she was holding for Margaret Judson.

Nancy studied them and thought, "There's no return address on any of them and they were mailed rather recently from Carrollton." Nancy knew this was a town not far from the hotel. She noted that much of the handwriting resembled Bartescue's autograph on her golf ball. "I'm sure he wrote all these letters," Nancy concluded.

Nancy's second stop was at the nearby college town of Andover. At the campus bookstore she asked to see the directory of instructors.

Rapidly Nancy searched through the list of professors for one whose first name was Mark. She felt highly elated when she came upon an instructor of philosophy named Mark Hilburn. Had she located Miss Judson's former fiancé? In scanning the rest of the list she discovered another Mark. His last name was Wardell. Was he the one?

"I guess I'll have to call on both men," Nancy decided.

Professor Hilburn was not in his office. She got his home address but wasted precious minutes trying to find the street.

Even before she rapped on the door of the neat little brick house Nancy suspected she was at the wrong place. An upset toy wagon on the front lawn gave mute evidence that Mark Hilburn was married. Mrs. Hilburn answered the bell. She proved to be a charming, middle-aged woman with three children.

"I shouldn't have troubled you," Nancy apologized. "The professor for whom I'm searching is single, and I know only his first name, which is Mark."

"Then the man you're looking for is Professor Mark Wardell," the woman suggested. "He's single and not more than thirty years old, I judge. He's the head of our zoology and botany departments."

"Can you tell me where he lives?" Nancy asked eagerly.

"His home is at 16 Hyman Street, and he has a housekeeper."

Ten minutes later Nancy rang the bell at the Wardell house. She was admitted by a pleasant woman.

"Professor Wardell isn't here just now," she replied to Nancy's inquiry. "Sometimes he comes home to lunch, but I never can be certain. He usually takes a hike in the woods. The professor is deeply interested in nature lore."

Nancy was disappointed but decided to take the woman into her confidence. She mentioned that she was trying to locate a man who was an acquaintance of Margaret Judson.

"Oh, dear me, they were more than mere acquaintances!" the housekeeper replied quickly. "Professor Wardell and Miss Judson were engaged. But no wedding took place. He hasn't seemed himself since."

Nancy was now convinced that Mark Wardell

was the person with whom she must talk if she expected to solve the mystery surrounding Margaret Judson.

"Will you please give Professor Wardell an important message," she requested and took a piece of paper from her purse. After writing her name and the address of her hotel on it, she handed over the notation.

"Ask him to see me at this address as soon as he can. It's extremely urgent."

"I'll be glad to. Are you a student here?" the woman asked.

"No."

On the way back to Deer Mountain Hotel, Nancy reflected that her morning had certainly been profitable. She thought, "It's rather a coincidence that both Professor Wardell and Mr. Haley are interested in botany and zoology. Is there a connection between the men?"

By the time she arrived at the hotel, Nancy barely had time to snatch a sandwich before she was due to appear at the first tee. Bess, George, Ned, and Mr. Drew were on hand to witness the start of the match, and smiled encouragingly as Nancy stood quietly awaiting her turn to drive off.

"Bring home the silver loving cup!" George urged in a whisper. "We'll be pulling for you!"

Betsy Howard, a well-known golfer, had turned in a score of seventy for her semifinal match, which was better than Nancy had ever made. The young detective knew that if she expected to win, she would have to turn in the best score of her life. Nancy feared that with her hand paining her, she might not even be able to play as well as usual.

"I'll do the best I can," she determined. "Win or lose, I'll accept the decision gracefully."

Miss Howard made a long drive from the tee. Nancy's ball did not go as far, but ended up in perfect position. When they reached the green, both putted well and the score was even.

The second and third holes were tied also. At the fourth hole Nancy gained the advantage when Miss Howard's ball lodged in a bunker, but the fifth hole found them even again. They played through the sixth and seventh, fighting for the lead.

So absorbed were both girls in their game that they scarcely noticed how overcast the sky had become. Black clouds rolled swiftly up from the west, blotting out the sun.

The ninth hole, marking the halfway point of the match, left the girls still even. Betsy Howard seemed as fresh as ever, and on the tenth tee drove out a ball which easily went two hundred and twenty yards.

"A beautiful drive," Nancy praised her as she stepped forward to take her turn.

She swung with all her strength, connecting

squarely with the ball, but at the same instant a severe pain shot through her injured hand. Nancy was suffering intensely, and it was all she could do to grip the club. As a result, her next shot was a dismal failure.

Quick to seize an advantage, Betsy Howard took the hole easily. The eleventh also fell to her. Nancy, two down, feared the match was lost.

"I can't give up," she said to herself grimly.

As the girls teed off at the twelfth hole, a few drops of rain spattered their faces. Betsy Howard glanced anxiously at the sky.

"It looks like a hard rain coming," she declared nervously. "I'm afraid of thunderstorms."

By the time the two reached the twelfth green, it was raining steadily. In trying to hurry, Betsy Howard missed her putt and the hole went to Nancy, leaving her now only one down. She must make up that point!

The thirteenth and fourteenth, played in a drenching downpour, were halved, leaving the score the same as before. By this time a rough wind had sprung up.

"This is terrible!" Betsy exclaimed. "Surely the committee can't expect us to finish our match in this kind of weather."

She hesitated a moment, then abruptly handed her driver to the caddy.

"I'm going back to the hotel," she announced.

"If the committee says we may continue the match tomorrow, fine. If not, then I'll default."

"No, we'll stop play by mutual agreement," Nancy replied. "No one would blame us for failing to finish under these conditions."

The rain began to fall in torrents. Betsy Howard, followed by the two caddies, ran as fast as she could toward the hotel. Nancy darted into the woods, and there, partly protected by the trees, made up her mind that the Haley cabin was closer than any other shelter.

The wind was rising steadily. As she ran through the woods, the tree boughs crashed together overhead. Near the haunted bridge, Nancy was startled to hear the same moaning and groaning sounds which the girls had noticed on their other visits. Then came a scream.

"That scream is from Mr. Haley's lion," she thought, "but what can be causing the other noises?"

Nancy approached the sagging bridge where the old scarecrow, wet and tattered, was dancing wildly in the wind. It seemed more ghostlike than ever. As the young sleuth hurried past, the spindly "arms" entwined themselves about her. But she shook herself free.

The bridge swayed in the wind. As Nancy reached midstream, it suddenly creaked. The underpinning had been torn away!

As the structure swung around, Nancy clutched the railing for support, but the decayed wood gave way. She was plunged forward into the turbulent waters of the swollen creek!

The current was swift. Before Nancy could battle her way to shore she found herself carried far beyond the place where the haunted bridge had stood. Her clothes were muddy and torn. She pulled herself out onto the slippery bank and sat there for a moment in the rain, trying to regain her breath.

"Bess warned me I'd get into trouble if I insisted upon coming here," she said to herself. "The old bridge had the last laugh."

Nancy's clothes were thoroughly soaked and her hair was plastered tightly against her head. She scrambled up the bank and followed the ravine trail to the cabin. Her firm knock brought Ned to the door.

"Why, Nancy, what happened to you?" he cried in astonishment. "I thought you were playing your golf match—"

Nancy grinned. "I was, but I decided to drop in for a moment and borrow an umbrella. Did you hear a loud crash a few minutes ago?"

"Yes, it sounded as if the bridge went down."

"It did. And I went with it. You should have seen me sailing down the ravine!"

An expression of concern remained on Ned's face in spite of the girl's bantering tone. "Your

Nancy was plunged into the turbulent stream!

hand, Nancy!" he exclaimed. "You've hurt it again!"

"It is swollen," she admitted. "But it'll be all right to finish the golf match tomorrow. We stopped because of the heavy rain."

Suddenly a thought came to Nancy. "Ned, I'm surprised to find you here. I thought you intended to stay at the hotel until the end of the golf match."

"I meant to, but just after you teed off, Burt came to tell me I was needed here again."

"Is Mr. Haley worse?" Nancy asked anxiously.

CHAPTER XIV

Surprise Visitor

"MR. HALEY has been very restless," Ned reported. "Burt and Dave are outside now trying to look after the mountain lion. I should be helping them."

"I'll stay here with Mr. Haley," Nancy said quickly. "You go ahead."

Before Ned could protest she had moved quietly to the adjoining bedroom. The patient was sleeping peacefully.

After Ned had donned a raincoat and left the cabin, Nancy tiptoed to a closet in search of warm garments. The only apparel available were a pair of slacks and an old blue shirt.

While she was hanging her own wet clothes by a lighted oil stove to dry she heard Mr. Haley tossing and hastened back to him. The man's eyes were wide open.

"Who are you?" he asked in a whisper.

"I am Nancy Drew, and I have come to help you."

She tried to explain the situation to him but Mr. Haley was too restless to listen. He raised himself on an elbow, motioning her to assist him from the bed.

"No, you must remain quiet," Nancy told him firmly. "You must not get up until the doctor says you may."

"But I have to! My lion will starve. How long have I been ill?"

"Now don't get excited," Nancy said soothingly. "Everything is all right. Your lion is being cared for by friends of mine. Just lie back and try to rest."

Presently Mr. Haley fell into a peaceful sleep. By the time Ned and the others came in, Nancy was able to report that she considered the patient well on the road to recovery.

"That's good news," Ned said in obvious relief. "By the way, you look great in Mr. Haley's clothes."

"I'll bet I do." She laughed.

As the storm subsided, the boys listened eagerly to her account of the day's golf match. Ned cheered Nancy by saying he was sure she would win the tournament. The other boys agreed.

After the rain ceased, Ned set off for the ravine with Burt and Dave to take a look at the fallen bridge. They found that it had floated some distance downstream and was lodged against an old log. They returned to the cabin for ropes and tools, saying they were going to try and pull the structure back into place and anchor it securely.

During the boys' absence Nancy donned her own clothes. Then, thoroughly worn out from her strenuous day, she sat down in a chair beside Mr. Haley and fell asleep.

She was awakened by a knock on the door and rose to open it. Before her stood a tall, handsome man who appeared to be about thirty years of age.

"I beg your pardon," he said politely. "Is Mr. Haley at home?"

"Yes, but I'm not sure he can see a visitor," Nancy replied. "He was injured in an accident and is in bed."

"Oh, who are you?" the stranger asked in alarm. "I had no idea anything was wrong here or I'd have come before this. Mr. Haley isn't in grave danger, is he?"

"He's recovering now."

"That's good," the caller said in relief. "Do you think I might see him? My name is Wardell and Mr. Haley is my uncle."

Nancy was taken completely by surprise. Recovering quickly, she invited the young man to come inside.

"Mr. Haley is sleeping now," she explained, "but when he wakes up he may be able to talk with you."

"I'd rather not if you feel it would excite him," Mr. Wardell said anxiously. "I think the world of my uncle. He practically reared me, and it was through him that I became interested in nature lore."

Nancy asked a few polite questions about Mr. Wardell's work. Although she knew that he was a professor at Andover College, she decided not to mention this immediately or reveal her identity.

"I came over to Deer Mountain Hotel this afternoon to see a young woman," he said. "She had requested me to call on an urgent matter. Apparently it couldn't have been very important, because she wasn't even there. Since I was near here I thought I'd drop over and see my uncle. Please tell me about the accident."

Nancy told him how she and her friends had discovered Mr. Haley. She wanted to bring Margaret Judson's name into the conversation but to do it as casually as possible.

"When Mr. Haley was injured, we were afraid he had no living relatives," she remarked. "There were no family photographs or other clues to their whereabouts. However, I did find a picture here in the cabin of a beautiful girl."

Nancy took out the photograph of Margaret Judson and handed it to Professor Wardell. He stared at it without speaking. An expression of deep anguish crossed his face.

"From something Mr. Haley said, I gathered that he knew this girl well," Nancy remarked. "Do you know her?"

"Could I ever forget her?" Wardell said with emotion. "Margaret Judson and I were engaged to be married, but—" The man's voice faltered.

Nancy watched with quiet sympathy as he fought to regain his composure.

The professor went on quickly. "I was away on a scientific expedition at the time Margaret's house was destroyed by fire. Everything in it was lost."

"Everything?" Nancy inquired.

"Well, she did save a chest of jewelry." Professor Wardell smiled grimly. "Among other things it contained the engagement ring I had given her."

"How fortunate!" Nancy murmured.

"It was anything but fortunate. In her escape Margaret lost the brass chest. She left a note for me at my uncle's cabin, saying that even though she loved me, she must break our engagement. I couldn't understand her actions then and I can't now. Why should she refuse to marry me just because the ring was lost? I'd be only too happy to buy Margaret another one.

"The ring was valuable, I admit," he went on, "but I'm sure Margaret knew me well enough to realize I wouldn't blame her for something that obviously wasn't her fault. People's tongues wagged. They said she set the blaze to collect the insurance. That was nonsense, because unfortunately the policy had lapsed. Oh, I hope nothing has happened to her."

Nancy was tempted to tell Professor Wardell she believed Miss Judson was in the vicinity of Deer Mountain. But before revealing any information about the young woman, she decided to consult her father.

"After you've visited your uncle a few minutes I want you to come with me to Deer Mountain Hotel," Nancy said, "and meet my father."

"I'll be delighted to talk with him," the professor said, "especially since I want to thank him for being so kind to my uncle. I must confess, however, that I don't know his name or yours either, for that matter."

Nancy enjoyed the man's look of astonishment as she replied with a smile, "I happen to be the girl who asked you to call at Deer Mountain Hotel. My name is Nancy Drew."

"You are Nancy Drew?" Professor Wardell exclaimed. "Why did you send for me?"

"I found something which I think may belong to Margaret Judson," she replied. "I can't tell you any more now. You must discuss it first with my father."

CHAPTER XV

Gathering Evidence

THE professor did not press Nancy for a further explanation. After they had conversed a few more minutes, he asked if he might see Mr. Haley now.

"Go right in." Nancy nodded toward the man's room.

Mr. Wardell found his uncle still asleep and returned to the living room.

Presently Ned, Burt, and Dave trudged in, exhausted by their attempt to repair the bridge. They told Nancy that while they had it anchored, considerable work would have to be done to make the bridge safe.

"You won't be able to cross the ravine to return to your hotel," Ned told her. "I'll drive you back."

"Thanks, Ned, but that won't be necessary. I want you to meet Professor Wardell." She pointed toward a dark corner of the room. "He has offered to take me in his car, which is parked at the Judson estate."

The stranger rose from a chair and came forward. As the boys were introduced, Ned glanced at the man with a puzzled look. He was wondering how Wardell had become acquainted with Nancy. Even her explanation that he was Mr. Haley's nephew did not lessen Ned's feeling of jealousy.

Nancy gave him a warm smile as if to reassure him. Then she asked Ned to take good care of the patient while she and the professor went to the hotel.

"I don't seem to be of much use at anything else," Ned muttered, turning away.

During the drive to Deer Mountain Hotel, Nancy told her companion more about her father. The professor said he was eager to meet the lawyer.

When they reached the lobby, Nancy said, "Will you, please, wait here while I go to Dad's room?"

He nodded and she went to the elevator. Nancy stopped a moment at George and Bess's room but the cousins were not there.

"Dad!" she cried, bursting in upon him. "I'm almost certain that the carved chest I found in the ravine is Miss Judson's missing property! I've brought Professor Wardell here. He's her former fiancé. I want you to talk to him."

Mr. Drew smiled. "You work fast, Nancy. I'd like very much to meet him." After hearing his daughter's full story, including the rained-out golf match, he said, "Bring Professor Wardell up to my room where we can talk privately."

Nancy hurried downstairs to get the professor. He and Mr. Drew immediately liked each other. Nancy listened tensely when her father broached the topic of his search for Miss Judson.

"I appreciate your opinion, sir," Professor Wardell said respectfully after he had listened to a summary of the evidence against the young woman. "But I cannot believe that Margaret knows anything about the jewel thefts. She was always so honorable and comes from a fine family. She couldn't possibly have any connection with a gang of thieves and smugglers."

"Nevertheless," said Mr. Drew, "there are a few clues which seem to connect her with the affair. For instance, one of the stolen items is a jeweled compact. We know that Miss Judson had one."

"That is not proof of her guilt," said the professor.

"Of course not," agreed Mr. Drew. "It could easily be coincidence."

Nancy spoke up. "Did you ever hear Miss Judson speak of Martin Bartescue?"

"Why yes. I believe she met him in Europe."

Nancy and her father exchanged quick glances.

"Is Bartescue under suspicion?" Wardell asked.

"Yes," Carson Drew answered gravely, "but so far the evidence against him is purely circumstantial. If only we could find Miss Judson, she might be able to clear up the mystery surrounding both of them."

"I have no idea where Margaret is," the professor replied. "She might be staying with a cousin in Rock City."

"You've never inquired?" Nancy asked in surprise.

"No," Wardell answered in a low tone. "I didn't want to force my attentions on Margaret. I don't feel I should seek her out deliberately without some indication on her part that she wants to see me again. I still believe, however, that if I could talk with her, everything might be explained and cleared up."

Professor Wardell arose to leave, saying he was already late for an important meeting.

"I'll be waiting eagerly to hear from you, Mr. Drew. Your daughter has my address at Andover. When I'm not there I usually can be reached at my office in the science building."

After he had gone, Nancy and her father discussed the case for a few minutes.

"In spite of all the evidence against Margaret Judson," said Nancy, "I have a hunch she is not involved with the jewel thieves. That's Mr.

Wardell's opinion and it's also yours, Dad, isn't it?"

"I hope that she will be cleared of suspicion." The lawyer smiled.

Presently Mr. Drew and his daughter gave up trying to figure out the puzzle. They turned their attention to another pressing matter. During Nancy's brief stay at Mr. Haley's cabin she had noticed that the food supply was low, and many articles were needed to make the patient and the boys more comfortable.

She suggested to her father that she, Bess, and George buy the necessary supplies and cook dinner for Ned and the others at the cabin.

"That's very thoughtful, Nancy. It will cheer them up a little. The boys haven't had much fun since they arrived."

Bess and George were still not in their room. Nancy searched the lobby and other places in and around the hotel where the cousins might be but could not find them.

She returned to Mr. Drew's room and told him that she could not locate Bess and George. "Would you like to go shopping with me?" she asked.

"Be glad to," the lawyer agreed. "I'll give you two minutes to change your clothes."

Ned was alone with Mr. Haley when she and her father reached the cabin. He explained that Burt and Dave were down at the ravine working on the footbridge. A short time later they returned, tired and hungry, but pleased to report that they had finished the repairs.

"Bess and George came down and watched for a while," Burt said. "They had planned to visit us at the cabin but couldn't get across the ravine. Nancy, they were concerned about you until we told them you were here during the storm. They went back to the hotel to find you and have dinner."

"And I came here to cook dinner for you!" Nancy chuckled. "I was so preoccupied with my shopping list I didn't even think to leave a note for Bess and George. They'll be disappointed when they find out."

Nancy began preparing a warm meal. Later the boys declared that it was the first really good cooking they had tasted since they had arrived.

After the dishes had been washed and put away, Mr. Drew said, "How would you fellows like to have the evening off? I'll be glad to stay here with Mr. Haley."

"That would be great!" Ned exclaimed. "Is there a dance at the hotel tonight, Nancy?"

"Yes. I imagine Bess and George would like some dates for it, too." She grinned.

"Then let's go!" Ned exclaimed. "Come on, fellows. We'll change our clothes right away."

While they were getting ready, Nancy and her

father sat with Mr. Haley in the adjoining room.

"How are you feeling?" Mr. Drew asked him gently when he saw that the patient's eyes were open.

"Better," he replied. "Only weak."

"That's to be expected," Nancy said soothingly. "You have been very ill. Later Dad will bring you some broth and toast."

She did not wish to excite Mr. Haley by further conversation, but he seemed to want her to talk. Finally Nancy went to the kitchen and took Miss Judson's photograph from the cupboard drawer, then returned to the sick man.

"Would you like me to place this picture near you where you can see it?" she inquired.

"Yes, please do," Mr. Haley answered. "Is Miss Margaret here now?"

"She does not know you've been ill."

"Then it was a dream—I thought she was seated beside me, holding my hand."

"Perhaps you confused me with Miss Judson," Nancy said quietly. "Tell me, did you work for her at the mansion?"

"Oh, yes. I took care of the trees and the garden and the flowers about the place. After Miss Margaret's parents died she didn't have much money but kept me on anyway."

Tears glistened in Mr. Haley's eyes and several moments elapsed before he spoke again.

"Miss Margaret was good and kind," he told his listeners. "She never once spoke a harsh word to me in all the years I knew her. That's why it hurt me to see her so unhappy."

"She was unhappy?" Nancy prompted as he fell silent again.

"Yes. After her parents died Miss Margaret was very lonely. She was to have been married, but the awful fire happened and all her plans were changed."

"In what way do you mean?" Carson Drew inquired.

"I don't know—" Mr. Haley murmured wearily.

"And you haven't seen her since the fire?" Nancy questioned softly.

"She came to my cabin twice—once to ask me to search for something she had lost. But I couldn't find it. I hunted everywhere. I told her that later and she never came here again."

Mr. Haley closed his eyes and turned his face toward the wall. Nancy and her father longed to ask him other questions but refrained. It was clear that the man was exhausted from talking.

Before Carson Drew and Nancy had a chance to discuss what Mr. Haley had told them, Ned, Burt, and Dave came into the bedroom.

"We're ready to leave, Nancy," Ned announced in a whisper.

"You all look handsome in your new outfits," she commented. The boys wore different colored striped sports jackets and dark-brown pants. "It's hard to tell who is the handsomest," she added.

"You'd better say Ned," Dave teased.

As the young people were driving away from the cabin in Ned's car he observed that Nancy was strangely silent.

"Is your hand bothering you?" he inquired anxiously.

"Not much," Nancy replied. "There's really nothing wrong with me, Ned. I was just thinking about Margaret Judson again. Ned, I *must* find her!"

"That's easier said than done."

"Yes, but I believe she's near here."

Ned glanced curiously at Nancy. Her next words astonished him even more, as with a quiet intensity in her voice, she added:

"It may sound silly to you, Ned, but I have a strange feeling—call it intuition if you will— that tonight I'll find Margaret Judson!"

"You seem very positive," Ned commented. "I certainly hope your hunch is right."

"Can you help me?" Nancy asked.

"I thought you didn't need my assistance," he replied impulsively.

"Oh, Ned, it was just that I couldn't explain everything to you about Mr. Wardell, and I'm afraid I can't even now. But sometime I'll be able to."

"That doesn't matter, Nancy. Just tell me what to do and I'll try to carry out orders."

"Ned, are you willing to substitute sleuthing for dancing tonight?"

CHAPTER XVI

The Hidden Note

MEANWHILE, at the Deer Mountain Hotel, George and Bess were wondering what had become of Nancy. They were pacing the lobby waiting for her. Finally she came in, and to their delight the three boys were with her.

"I didn't mean to worry you," Nancy apologized to the cousins. "I jumped from one thing to another so fast I forgot to leave word where I was going to be."

Bess and George were enthusiastic to have their favorite dates take them to the dance, and promptly forgave Nancy for the anxiety she had caused them.

The two girls hurried to their rooms to change. Ned, Burt, and Dave sat down in the lobby, while Nancy went to the desk to inquire for mail.

"Any letters for me?" she asked.

The desk clerk handed her two envelopes. One

was plain, the other bore the hotel insigne. Nancy decided instantly that the latter was from Bartescue. She opened it and was not mistaken. It said:

I won my golf match today and hope the rain did not cause you to lose yours. Important business calls me away from the hotel, but I hope to see you before you return home.

"Important business," Nancy mused as she tucked the letter into her pocket. "I wonder if it concerns Margaret Judson!"

She opened the second letter, and was astonished to learn that it was from the young woman she hoped to find that night. The typed message and signature read:

The bearer of this note said that you wish to see me. Please write your message and leave it tonight before nine o'clock in one hand of the fountain statue.

Margaret Judson

Nancy read the note a second time to be sure that she had fully absorbed its amazing contents, then turned to the desk clerk.

"Can you tell me who delivered this letter?"

"I was not on duty at the time, Miss Drew."

Nancy wondered if the messenger could have been Bartescue. She would have to wait and ask the day clerk when he came on duty.

By this time Bess and George had returned.

Before they went off with Burt and Dave, Nancy told them about the two notes. Afterward she showed Ned the one from Margaret Judson.

He grinned. "It looks as if your hunch is correct, Nancy. You may meet the mysterious lady before the evening is over."

"Ned, let's walk into the garden. I need a moment to figure out what to do. I'm not certain which statue Miss Judson means. It's probably the large one at the rear of the hotel. I think that's the only statue connected with a fountain."

"Let's look," Ned suggested.

Without appearing to be particularly interested in the surroundings, the couple walked slowly about the hotel grounds. Finally they stopped at the fountain, pretending to watch the goldfish in its basin.

"I've decided to leave a blank sheet of paper here, Ned. I would write a note but I'm a little suspicious Margaret Judson didn't send me that letter."

"You think it's a forgery?"

"It could be. I'd like to compare Miss Judson's signature with the one on Mr. Haley's photograph, but I won't have time now to go back to the cabin."

Ned looked at his watch. "No, I guess you won't. It's almost nine o'clock."

"We must work quickly. Wait here, Ned, please."

Nancy ran back into the hotel, but soon reappeared with a folded paper in her hand. The couple sat down on a nearby bench and waited until the grounds were deserted. Then Ned leaned across the stone basin of the fountain and placed the sheet of paper in the upraised hand of the marble figure.

"Now we'll act as if we're returning to the hotel," Nancy whispered.

"Later," said Ned, "we can sneak back here to see if anyone comes for the message."

They retraced their steps to the hotel, walked through the lobby, and left by a side door. Selecting a bench which was screened from the fountain by huge bushes, they stationed themselves to wait.

Nine o'clock came, and no one appeared to take the message. An hour later a couple strolled past the fountain, but did not reach for the note.

"I'm beginning to think my piece of paper will never be claimed," Nancy said with a sigh. "Ned, will you do me another favor?"

"You know I will."

"This may sound silly, but I'd like you to drive me to the vicinity of Hemlock Hall."

Nancy was convinced by this time that Margaret Judson was not coming to the Deer Mountain Hotel. She suspected that the mysterious note had been written by Bartescue.

"Haven't you searched for Miss Judson at Hemlock Hall before?" Ned asked Nancy as the two rode along.

"Yes, but tonight I have a new idea. Maybe Margaret Judson has rented a home near the hotel. But she comes to Hemlock Hall once in a while. I want to interview various real-estate agents."

"But their offices will be closed, Nancy."

"I know, but we'll call at their homes. Oh, Ned, I *must* find Margaret Judson tonight!"

Nancy set out with high hopes of calling on every real-estate agent in the small city of Crofton. As they tried one man after another, she learned nothing. Finally Nancy interviewed John Spencer, the last agent on her list.

"Why, yes," he replied. "I rented a furnished house only this morning to a Miss Judson but I can't recall her first name."

When Nancy convinced him that the matter was of vital importance the realtor obligingly agreed to accompany the couple to his office. He and Nancy went inside. Mr. Spencer checked his records.

"Yes," he said, "the house at 508 Elmwood Street was taken by a Margaret Judson. She signed a six-months' lease."

Nancy thanked him as she wrote down the address and how to find it. Then she hurried back to the car. The agent had given such precise directions for reaching Elmwood Street that Ned had no difficulty in locating the house. To Nancy's disappointment it was in darkness.

"Perhaps Miss Judson has gone to bed," Ned suggested, halting the car on the opposite side of the street.

"It's possible she hasn't moved in yet," Nancy remarked.

"Suppose I run across the street and try the bell," Ned offered.

As he started to open the car door, Nancy suddenly tugged his arm.

"Wait!" she whispered tensely.

A car with brilliant headlights came slowly down the street. The woman driver swung into the gravel driveway at 508.

"That must be Margaret Judson!" Nancy said excitedly. "After she's inside we'll knock."

They watched the shadowy figure leave the car and enter the large white house. Soon the lower floor was flooded with light. The young woman closed the window blinds.

"Shall we go now?" Nancy suggested.

She and Ned went to the front door and pressed the doorbell. Presently they heard footsteps.

CHAPTER XVII

Big Mistake

"HERE comes Miss Judson," Nancy whispered. "If she proves to be the one we want, let's not tell her the real purpose of our visit."

The door opened, and the same young woman Nancy had spoken to at Hemlock Hall peered out.

"Miss Judson?" Nancy asked.

"Yes."

As a beam of light fell directly on the girl's face, the young woman added, "Oh, I remember you. We met at Hemlock Hall. Do come in."

Nancy introduced Ned and herself. The three walked into the colonial furnished living room and seated themselves.

"I'm afraid I have rather distressing news to report," Nancy said. "I'm staying at Deer Mountain Hotel and became acquainted with a man who formerly worked at your estate."

"Not Joe Haley?" Margaret Judson asked quickly.

"Yes. Mr. Haley was injured in an accident." Nancy told the woman what had happened. "He mentioned you and pleaded to see you."

"Oh, I must go to him at once!" Margaret cried. "What hospital is he in?"

"Mr. Haley is at his cabin in the woods," Nancy explained. "The doctor did not think it necessary to move him."

"Then I shall go there!" the young woman exclaimed. Suddenly a startled expression came over her face. "No, I can't go after all," she murmured.

"I'm sorry," Nancy said. "Mr. Haley really needs you."

"I want to go—you don't understand. I'm just afraid I might meet a certain person there."

"Mark Wardell?" Nancy questioned.

Margaret Judson buried her face in her hands and sobbed.

"Yes, yes, he's the one. How can I face him while I am regarded as a thief!"

Nancy crossed the room and put an arm around the young woman. "Please don't cry," she said soothingly.

Meanwhile, Bess and George were enjoying the dance at Deer Mountain Hotel with Burt and Dave.

"The dancing will soon be over," Bess declared

anxiously as she gazed about the ballroom. "What can be keeping Nancy and Ned?"

Before anyone could hazard a guess, a boy came through the ballroom, calling George Fayne's name. The girls motioned to him, hoping that Nancy had sent a note to explain her absence.

"You're wanted on the telephone, Miss Fayne," the boy told her.

"I can't imagine who would call me here," she murmured. "I don't believe it's from Nancy. It might be from home."

Her guess was right. Mrs. Fayne in River Heights, lonesome for the sound of her daughter's voice, had telephoned merely to inquire if George was all right.

"Oh, yes, Mother, and we're having a fantastic time here. I wrote to you today."

At this point George lost the thread of conversation completely, because in the adjoining booth she heard the excited voice of a man saying:

"So the guy is a forger! He skipped out!"

"Did you hear what I said?" Mrs. Fayne questioned her daughter anxiously. "Your—"

"Oh, yes, that's nice," George replied hastily, her mind on the conversation in the other booth.

"Those two B-A-R's look alike?" she heard the man ask. "And you say the M and the T are similar? . . . Yes, I agree that ought to be enough to convict him."

George's mind worked with lightning-like speed. B-A-R were the first three letters of Martin Bartescue's last name and there was an M and a T in his first name. The man was a forger just as Nancy had suspected! The person in the next booth very likely was a hotel official who was being told of the discovery.

"George," came her mother's voice in exasperation, "what is the matter with you?"

"I—I can't talk now," George stammered. "Something important has come up. I'll call back a little later."

She hung up and darted from the phone booth. The adjoining one was now empty. Since Nancy was not available, George hurried to tell Bess, Burt, and Dave what had happened.

"I've just made an important discovery," she revealed. "Bartescue definitely is a forger and apparently the hotel people are on to him!"

"No wonder he skipped out!" Bess exclaimed. "That explains the note he left Nancy. He's probably miles away by now."

"But he's supposed to play his final golf match tomorrow," said George. "Let's walk down to the caddy house and find out if his clubs are gone."

"I'll bet," Dave spoke up, "that he won't show up for the golf match if he's facing arrest."

"Let's find out anyway."

The two couples walked across the grounds toward the caddy house, clearly outlined in the moonlight. The shack had been locked for the night. Disappointed, they turned toward the hotel.

Suddenly Burt noticed an object gleaming in the grass and stooped to pick it up. "Someone's keys."

"One of the golfers, I suppose," said George. "We can turn the keys in at the office."

Burt dropped them into his pocket, and the four friends walked on toward the hotel. As they came within view of the garden, George abruptly halted, clutching Burt's arm.

"Look! Over toward that statue by the fountain! It's Barty! Bess, let's you and I sneak up there."

While the boys waited, the girls crept forward, taking care to keep themselves hidden by bushes and trees. They saw him reach across the basin of the fountain and remove a white object from the hand of the statue.

"It must have been a note from someone," George said in an undertone. "Bess, we must capture him!"

"We can't do that alone."

"No, we must get Burt and Dave!"

Quietly the girls hurried back. The boys were eager to help.

"Tell us what to do."

"Capture that man," Bess whispered.

The four quietly approached the fountain.

Bartescue was standing there, studying a sheet of paper in his hand. They heard him mutter something, then he crumpled the paper and hurled it angrily into the pool.

"Now's our chance!" Burt whispered.

Stealthily the boys moved forward. There was bright moonlight. Suddenly Bartescue turned his head. Sensing the boys' intent, he gave a cry of alarm and fled toward the caddy house.

"Don't let him get away!" Dave cried as the young people gave chase.

Burt, who was a champion sprinter on the Emerson College track team, soon overtook the man and threw him to the ground. The others closed in so the prisoner could not escape.

"What's the meaning of this outrage?" Barty demanded, furious. "Let me up."

"We'll release you when the police come," Dave retorted grimly. "You low-down forger!"

"I've never forged anything in my life," Bartescue denied in a rasping tone. Burt and Dave soon discovered that it was not easy to keep the strong and agile man pinned to the ground.

George glanced quickly toward the caddy house. Inspired by a sudden thought, she asked Burt for the keys he had found and ran to the locked door to try them. One fit perfectly and she was able to unlock the door.

Bartescue was thrust inside and the door securely locked again. Burt and Dave said they

"Don't let him get away!" Dave cried

would stand guard while the girls ran back to the hotel to notify the officials.

"Let me out of here!" Barty yelled at the top of his lungs, pounding savagely on the door. "You have no right to do this!"

In the meantime Bess and George had reached the hotel. Greatly excited, they hurried to the manager's office and burst in upon him.

"Come quickly!" George cried. "We've captured your forger!"

"What!" the manager demanded incredulously. "You've caught the man?"

"Yes, we have him—in the caddy house! Follow us."

Bess and George were glowing with pride by the time they came to it. There was not a sound within. Apparently Bartescue had decided that it was useless to try convincing the boys of his innocence. Bess unlocked the door and the manager cautiously peered inside.

"Come out of there, you!" he ordered sharply.

Disheveled, Bartescue haughtily emerged from the building. He glared at Bess and George, then cast an accusing glance at the hotel manager.

"Sir, I demand an explanation for this outrageous treatment. Never before in my life have I been so abused and insulted!"

The manager had not spoken a word. He could only stare.

"Oh, Mr. Bartescue, this is all a mistake," he said finally.

"A mistake!" George exclaimed indignantly. "This man is a forger. I heard you say so your-self when you were talking in a telephone booth. Or at least I thought it was you."

"It's not Martin Bartescue who is wanted for forgery," the manager said.

"But the letters B-A-R—"

"They stand for Barney. One of our newly em-ployed cooks, a man by the name of Jennings, forged a hundred-dollar check. He used the sig-nature of Barney Milton, who is our caddy mas-ter. Mr. Bartescue had nothing whatever to do with the matter."

George murmured in confusion, "I shouldn't have acted so impulsively, only I thought Mr. Bartescue was under suspicion even before this. He has written his name so many different ways."

"I can explain that," Barty said coldly.

"Then please do," Bess insisted.

"I shall explain nothing to you," the man re-torted. "When Miss Drew comes I will tell her—in private!"

He turned and walked toward the hotel. The manager hastened after him, continuing to offer apologies for the mistake.

"I seem to have achieved the prize boo-boo," George said contritely.

"But the fact remains," Bess agreed soberly, "that Bartescue still has a lot to explain."

"We must find Nancy immediately," George declared urgently. "Barty may slip away, and then we'll never learn the reason for his strange actions."

CHAPTER XVIII

Exonerated

FOLLOWING Margaret Judson's plaintive announcement that she could not face her former fiancé, Nancy tried to draw the full story from the young woman. Margaret said again that it was because she had been accused of being a thief.

"But you're innocent, aren't you?" Ned asked.

"Oh, yes, yes. I have never done anything dishonest in my life. And please forgive my tears," Margaret Judson replied in embarrassment.

Finding Nancy and Ned sympathetic, the young woman began to explain the situation.

"It happened a little over two years ago," she said. "On the way home from a trip abroad I met a charming woman named Mrs. Brownell and we became good friends. I finally invited her to spend a weekend at my home."

"Your house near Deer Mountain Hotel?" Nancy asked.

"Yes. I was living there at the time. Mrs.

Brownell accepted my invitation. One evening before dinner I learned that my guest loved beautiful jewelry. I opened the safe and showed her a small chest containing my family heirlooms. Instead of returning it to the safe, as I should have done, I placed the chest in my bureau drawer.

"That night as I was preparing for bed, Mrs. Brownell came to my room to show me a jeweled compact. It was exquisite. We chatted for a time, then she went back to her room. Later I noticed she had left the compact on my dresser."

"You didn't attempt to return it to her?" Nancy asked in surprise.

"Mrs. Brownell had retired before I realized she'd left it, so I put the compact in the chest. I meant to give it to her early in the morning. Fire broke out during the night.

"It seemed to be everywhere at once. When I awoke, my bedroom was filled with smoke, and flames were shooting up the stairway. I ran to Mrs. Brownell's room and awakened her. By then it was too late to save very much, and we were forced to escape down a porch trellis."

"Did you forget the box of jewelry?" Nancy asked.

"No, I wrapped it in some of my clothing. Then I snatched up my pocketbook and managed to escape just an instant before the floor of my room crashed. In terror, I ran toward Joe Haley's cabin.

"Somehow I got lost. I remember stumbling across the ravine bridge, but my memory about what happened after that isn't very clear. Apparently I wandered through the woods until I blacked out. In any event, hours elapsed before I recovered consciousness. I was chilled to the bone.

"When I looked about, the bundle of clothing and my pocketbook were still beside me. The little chest of jewelry with Mrs. Brownell's compact was gone."

"Where was Mrs. Brownell?" Ned put in.

"I don't know. I'm not sure if she followed me across the bridge."

"Did you notice footprints when you woke up? Which way did they go?" Nancy queried.

Margaret Judson shook her head. "I was too excited to notice anything. I wandered about in a semi-dazed condition, hoping I'd find the jewelry. It seemed certain I must have dropped it somewhere in the woods.

"When dawn came I knew that the search was useless and I was exhausted. I staggered to Mr. Haley's cabin and told him about the fire and that I'd lost the chest. I begged him to try to find it. He promised he would."

"Was the jewelry extremely valuable?" Ned asked.

"Yes, several of the pieces were priceless. Among them was my diamond engagement ring.

I valued it more than anything else. And, of course, Mrs. Brownell's jeweled compact was worth a small fortune."

"According to her estimate," Nancy remarked. "Did you agree?"

"She came to see me later and said it was valued at six thousand dollars. I wouldn't know its worth," Margaret answered. "She blamed me entirely for the loss."

"How could she do that when she left the compact on your dresser?" Ned spoke up.

Margaret shrugged. "Mrs. Brownell demanded that I return it immediately or pay her the amount. She threatened to turn me over to the police. I would have paid the money gladly but I couldn't afford to. I had only a small bank account. Nearly everything I owned except a few acres of land was destroyed in the fire. Unfortunately the insurance policy on the property had lapsed."

Nancy said thoughtfully, "I doubt that she could have proved any claim against you."

"You mean she couldn't have had me arrested?"

"I don't think so."

"She would have said that I had hidden the jewel case deliberately."

"Even so, Mrs. Brownell couldn't have won her case without proof," Ned told her. "You should have consulted a lawyer."

"I realize that now, but at the time I was

panic-stricken. I ran away and lived for a while in Chicago."

"Running away was the worst thing you could have done," Ned remarked.

"I was so upset I acted impulsively. All along I kept hoping Joe Haley would find the jewel chest. It had to be somewhere in the woods. So much time has passed now, that of course there's no hope of finding it."

"Don't give up yet," Nancy remarked, but the young woman did not seem to hear her.

"Mrs. Brownell has never stopped bothering me since the compact was lost," Margaret Judson went on. "While she has never come to me herself, she has sent a friend."

"A friend?" Nancy inquired.

"Another woman, who follows me wherever I go. She keeps pressing me for money and threatening that unless I pay she will expose me to my friends and to the police."

"Margaret, I think your troubles are nearly over," Nancy said kindly. "Your jewel box has been found."

"What!" The young woman trembled with eagerness. "Did Joe Haley find it?"

"No, it came into my possession by accident," Nancy explained. "Tell me, what was the little chest made of?"

"Carved brass, and the design was very beautiful. It's hard to describe, but—I can draw it."

Margaret Judson made a rough sketch that convinced Nancy the chest she had found in the ravine did indeed belong to the young woman.

"Did it contain the missing compact?" Margaret asked anxiously.

"Yes, and the diamond ring you mentioned. I think everything that was in the chest the night of the fire is still there."

"Oh, Nancy, how can I ever thank you?"

Smiling, Nancy suggested, "Perhaps you'd like to go to the cabin now. Mr. Haley would be happy to see you again."

As the car sped along the road toward Deer Mountain, Nancy answered the young woman's questions concerning the discovery.

Margaret knit her brow. "Could I have dropped it on the bank of the stream when I crossed the bridge that terrible night? I have no recollection of anything I did."

"It's possible the chest slipped from the bundle of clothing you put it in," Nancy agreed. "I found it buried deep in the mud."

Ned parked the car at the side of the road. The three walked along the trail to the cabin. From a distance they could see lights glimmering through the trees. As they approached closer they heard men's voices.

Nancy assumed that her father was talking with Mr. Haley, and she felt elated to think that the patient was gaining steadily in strength.

The sound of footsteps brought Carson Drew to the door. As he flung it open, Nancy glanced inside and saw that her father had a visitor. She looked at Margaret Judson.

Directly behind Mr. Drew stood Mark Wardell!

Margaret did not see her former fiancé until after she had entered the lighted cabin. Their eyes met in a surprised stare. Neither spoke.

An awkward silence followed. Even Nancy could think of nothing to say or do at such a critical moment.

CHAPTER XIX

A Match of Wits

At last Mark Wardell took a step toward his former fiancée.

"Margaret," he murmured.

"Mark," she replied and with a little sob threw herself into his arms. "I've missed you so very much."

Mr. Drew, Nancy, and Ned decided that the happy reunion should be private. They slipped quietly into Mr. Haley's bedroom and closed the door.

"If Margaret and Mark can just talk things over alone," Nancy whispered to her father and Ned, "I'm sure everything will turn out perfectly."

"This plan of yours to reunite the lovers is fine," Carson Drew replied gravely, "but don't forget the stolen compact that was found in Margaret Judson's brass chest."

Nancy laughingly pressed her fingers against her father's lips.

"Wait, Dad, until you've heard my story. I'm positive Margaret is innocent! She explained the whole matter to our satisfaction." Ned nodded in agreement.

"I'd like to hear what she said," the lawyer replied.

With a word now and then from Ned, Nancy related what she had learned from Margaret Judson. She was gratified to see that the information seemed to impress her father.

"In my opinion," Nancy said, "Mrs. Brownell and her mysterious friend are the suspects in this case," she ended.

"You may be right, Nancy," her father commented, "but—"

There was no opportunity to say more just then because the door opened. Margaret and Mark stood there, smiling. They did not need to announce that their engagement had been renewed.

"I'll never be able to repay you for your kindness," Margaret told Nancy, tears gleaming in her eyes. "Ask any favor—"

"I have just one. Talk with my father about Mrs. Brownell and her friend, and give him as much information about them as you can remember."

Mr. Haley, who had been sleeping soundly,

stirred restlessly. Margaret Judson stepped forward to take the man's hand in her own.

"Is that you, Miss Margaret?" he asked.

"Yes," she answered softly. "You must try to get well."

The man's eyes roved over her lovely face. "I am so glad you came. But I have failed you. I tried. I could not find the box of jewels."

"It doesn't matter now. The chest has been found so don't worry any more."

With a sigh of relief the man closed his eyes and fell into a restful sleep. While Ned remained at the bedside, Mr. Drew and Nancy led Margaret Judson to the living room.

"I have no idea what became of Mrs. Brownell," the young woman reported, "but her friend, Mrs. Cartlett, annoyed me a few days ago at Hemlock Hall. I think perhaps she's staying there."

"Will you try to get in touch with her tomorrow?" Mr. Drew asked.

"Yes," the other answered.

Carson Drew decided to take Margaret Judson into his confidence and explained that he wished to locate the two women in order to set a trap for Mrs. Brownell.

"If you are able to reach Mrs. Cartlett," he said, "inform her that you have recovered the jewelry. Tell her to notify her friend that she must meet you at the cabin if she wishes to get back the lost compact."

"I'm almost afraid to see Mrs. Brownell alone," Margaret admitted. "She has a violent temper."

"Perhaps I could come here with you," Nancy suggested. Then as a second thought occurred to her she added, "Oh, I forgot about the tournament tomorrow."

Mr. Drew smiled at his daughter. "I believe I can arrange matters for you so your match can be played in the afternoon. The tournament chairman is very reasonable. By the way, Nancy, how's your hand?"

"It's better, Dad. I haven't felt much pain in it today."

A few minutes later Margaret Judson, her fiancé, Nancy, and Mr. Drew prepared to drive to Deer Mountain Hotel. The engaged couple had decided to take rooms there until the mystery was cleared up.

As Nancy said good-by to Ned, she remarked, "As usual, you seem to be the one who must hold the fort. Hope you're not too bored."

"No chance," Ned told her. "Besides plenty of excitement, I've found some fascinating books here on wildlife."

At the hotel Nancy was greeted by her friends with a flood of questions.

"We were worried sick over you," said Bess.

She and the others were introduced and told the amazing turn of events. They congratulated the reunited couple.

Margaret was able to get a room near Nancy's. When they reached it, Nancy lingered a few minutes to talk.

"I don't wish to be personal," she began, "but are you well acquainted with a man named Martin Bartescue?"

"No," Margaret replied promptly. "I met him on my trip abroad, but I didn't care for him."

"Have you seen him since your return to this country?"

"Oh, no. He was just a casual acquaintance."

Nancy said, "Mr. Bartescue has been staying at this hotel. He pretended to know you well."

"Mrs. Brownell knew the man very well," Margaret said thoughtfully. "It was through her that I met him. Later she told him where I lived. But I did not want to encourage him to contact me and told her so."

Nancy remembered the telegram Bartescue had intended for Margaret Judson. "He decided not to send it," the young detective thought, "because deep down he knew she would not answer."

Margaret looked so weary Nancy said good night and went to Bess and George's room to hear about their evening. The cousins related their adventure with Martin Bartescue.

"Don't feel bad about your mistake, George." Nancy chuckled. "It served him right. He thought he would play a joke on me by asking me to leave a message in one hand of the statue."

"I still think Barty must be a crook," George insisted. "Otherwise, how do you explain his different styles of handwriting?"

Nancy's answer surprised Bess and George. "I think he's just a practical joker. He thinks it's fun to keep us mystified."

"Hm!" said George in disgust.

In the morning Nancy learned from the tournament chairman that her golf match had been postponed until one o'clock. That left the young people ample time to attend church and for Margaret to telephone Mrs. Brownell's friend Mrs. Cartlett at Hemlock Hall.

The conversation between the two was brief. Mrs. Cartlett agreed to come to the cabin in the woods at five o'clock, bringing Mrs. Brownell with her.

"Everything is working out according to Dad's plan," Nancy declared in delight.

After they had finished eating, the group started for the golf course.

"I can't wait for the confrontation at the cabin," Nancy said to Margaret. "I only hope my golf match won't keep me from witnessing the grand finale to the mystery."

"Oh, it mustn't!" Margaret exclaimed. "If we have a few minutes to spare on the way to the cabin, Nancy, I'd like to stop at my house and pick up a few clothes. I have nothing at Deer Mountain Hotel, and I'd like to dress up a bit."

"For Mark?" Nancy teased.

"Yes," the young woman said, blushing.

"I don't blame you," Nancy replied, but she added soberly, "I hope everything turns out as well as we expect."

Margaret glanced at her in alarm. "Will I be cleared of the accusation against me?"

"No doubt about it. We'll make Mrs. Brownell confess!" Nancy said confidently.

It occurred to her, however, that if Mrs. Brownell should get the slightest inkling she was under suspicion, the woman would not keep the appointment at Mr. Haley's cabin.

Since it was nearly one o'clock, Nancy hurried to meet Betsy Howard on the golf course.

Coming toward her was Barty, who had just finished his final match. From the dour expression on his face she gathered he had not won the men's championship.

"How did you come out in your game?" she asked.

"I lost," he snapped. "I blame it on those two friends of yours, too!"

"What did they have to do with it?"

"I was so upset by everything that happened last night I couldn't get a grip on myself. My swing was all off."

"That's too bad," Nancy replied.

As she started to walk on, Bartescue attached himself to her, eager to talk.

"I told your friends I'd explain everything to you and to you only," he declared. "I was aware all along that you are the famous girl detective Nancy Drew. I made up my mind to match wits with you," Bartescue went on. "I guess I fooled you too, didn't I?"

"For a few days," Nancy answered. "I admit I suspected you of being a forger."

"Because of my handwriting?"

"Yes, but you changed the style of your signature a bit too often. It became obvious you were trying to confuse me."

"Years ago in college I discovered I had the ability to simulate varying styles of handwriting and I've had a lot of fun doing it occasionally."

"It seems to me like a dangerous pastime," Nancy remarked. "You may find yourself in trouble with the law."

"Oh, I can take care of myself," Barty chuckled. "Well, young lady, run along since you seem to be in such a hurry. After you win your match, I'll buy you a 2 B X Gardenia!"

Laughing heartily at his own joke, he walked on toward the hotel.

"The conceit of that man!" Nancy muttered. "When I called him he made up that phony 2 B X Gardenia code and there's nothing to it!"

Nancy greeted Betsy Howard and walked with her to the fifteenth tee where play was to be resumed. A large crowd of spectators had followed the two players and Nancy's friends had joined the crowd.

"Good luck!" George called.

It was generally conceded that Betsy would win the match and thus the tournament. Being one point ahead with only four holes left to play, she held the advantage. Then, too, because of Nancy's injured hand, few persons believed she could play her best game.

Betsy Howard, having won the last hole, held the honor of driving first and sent a long, straight ball flying down the fairway. Undaunted, Nancy teed up and swung her club with all her strength. Since they were nearing the end of the match, she had no intention of babying her injured hand.

Nancy had struck her ball squarely. To her satisfaction it sailed past the trees and came to rest in the middle of the fairway some yards ahead of Betsy's drive. A murmur of admiration ran through the crowd.

As Nancy was leaving the tee, her caddy followed. On a sudden inspiration she asked, "Chris, have you ever caddied for Mr. Bartescue?"

"Yes, Miss Drew. Why?"

While she was trying to decide how to find out if the man had ever quizzed the caddy about her interest in the haunted bridge, he replied to her unspoken question.

"Mr. Bartescue was always asking me where I thought you went. I never told him about the—

the scarecrow." The boy laughed. "All I said was that you seemed interested in Miss Margaret Judson who used to live near here."

At that moment the conversation was interrupted by a boy from the hotel. He handed Nancy a sealed letter. Promptly she tore open the envelope.

A broad smile spread over the girl's face as she read the message: "Good luck, Nancy. The stage is set for Mrs. Brownell's arrival."

Nancy smiled. Her darling father! He did not overlook a thing. She knew he had been in touch with New York detectives asking that they bring the stolen compact with them. Undoubtedly he was now awaiting their arrival at the airport.

"Everything is moving along, so there's nothing for me to worry about except this golf match!" Nancy reflected, studying her next shot.

She addressed the ball. While the crowd watched in admiration, Nancy made a beautiful drive which her opponent could not equal. She won the hole, squaring the match.

Betsy Howard, grimly determined not to lose the tournament, wasted no shots on the sixteenth hole, with the result she matched Nancy's strokes equally. With only two holes to be played, the score still stood even.

As Nancy prepared to make her first shot from the seventeenth tee, Chris sidled up to her. "Miss Drew," he said timidly, taking a ball from his pocket, "I don't know if this is the right time to tell you, but see what I found!"

"The ball Jimmy Harlow autographed for me! Thanks a lot!" Nancy cried in delight. "Where was it?"

"Not far from the haunted bridge. It was hidden under some dry leaves. Why don't you finish the tournament with the autographed ball? It may bring you luck."

Nancy crossed her fingers and smiled. "I'd like to use it." Turning to her opponent she requested permission to change balls.

"I have no objection," Betsy assured her.

Nancy felt confident as she teed up the Jimmy Harlow ball. Had it not led her straight to an absorbing mystery? Could it also help her win the silver trophy?

CHAPTER XX

A Day to Remember

NANCY was so intent on her golf game she hardly noticed the pain in her hand. She became oblivious to the crowd and their comments. She was not aware that her excellent shots were forcing Betsy Howard to "press" and make costly errors.

After Nancy putted at the seventeenth green she vaguely heard Chris say, "You're one up, Miss Drew! Halve this hole and the women's championship is yours!"

Nancy played the eighteenth in true championship style, every shot straight and true. Betsy, in a desperate attempt to win, had tried too hard. She had sent her ball into a sand trap, costing her an extra point. Nancy's ball already rested about ten yards from the cup.

After Betsy chipped her ball onto the green, she was eight feet from the hole. Nancy putted her ball with care and confidence. It rolled so swiftly that a little gasp of horror went up from the crowd. Many thought it would end at the far side of the green. But the ball had been tapped accurately and it dropped into the cup.

Betsy Howard stood perfectly still for a moment. Then she putted her own ball, missed, and tried again. This time it dropped, but already the match was lost. She reached out and grasped Nancy's hand.

"Congratulations, my dear. You played a beautiful game."

The crowd cheered, and friends rushed forward to praise Nancy. She smiled happily and thanked them. Then she was led in triumph to the hotel and received the handsome silver trophy for the women's championship.

"We knew you'd do it!" Bess cried gaily. "Oh, Nancy, you were marvelous!"

"Your score today was sixty-nine," George added proudly. "It sets a new record for women at the Deer Mountain course. And you were the youngest one in the tournament, too!"

Nancy grinned, then whispered, "Will you do me a favor?" George and Bess nodded.

"Please put this trophy in my room. I'd like to get to the cabin before Mrs. Brownell arrives."

"Margaret decided to leave before you," Bess told her. "She thought you wouldn't mind. Your father wanted her to be at the cabin early."

As Nancy hastened alone toward the woods she could not help reflecting that it was a pity Mrs. Brownell chose to live by dishonest means. She caught herself wondering about the child's picture in the jeweled compact. Who was she?

Nancy's thoughts were interrupted as she approached the bridge. Moaning and groaning filled the air, louder than ever, and the scarecrow danced wildly in the wind.

Nancy stopped in the middle of the bridge and gazed up into the tossing treetops, listening carefully. Suddenly she gave a little smile, and with a nod of satisfaction, hurried on.

She made her way quietly along the familiar path to the cabin. Hearing no voices within, she opened the door. Carson Drew sprang to his feet, then laughed in relief as he saw that the caller was his daughter.

"I thought for a moment Mrs. Brownell had caught me napping. Did you win the game?"

"Yes. Did you get the compact?" Nancy asked.

Mr. Drew nodded. "I've given it to Margaret Judson. The detectives who brought it are hidden outside with the federal agents. In fact, there are men stationed all along the roads from her hotel. Should Mrs. Brownell decide not to come here or try to flee from us after being accused of the theft, she'll find every avenue of escape cut off."

"You're convinced of her guilt, Dad?"

"Yes. New York authorities now have evidence

which I think will convict her. We want Margaret Judson's positive identification, however."

The young woman was with Mr. Haley, but at the lawyer's suggestion she came to the living room and sat down by a window. The others secreted themselves in a closet.

Fifteen minutes elapsed, and both Nancy and her father were growing weary of their cramped quarters. Suddenly they heard Margaret say in an excited undertone:

"Mrs. Brownell is coming now. And Mrs. Cartlett's with her!"

Margaret opened the cabin door to admit the two women. They glanced about quickly. Then, apparently satisfied that no trap had been set for them, addressed Miss Judson.

"I am in a great hurry," Mrs. Brownell said. "My friend tells me you have recovered the jeweled compact."

"I have it here," Margaret replied, "but I must be certain that it belongs to you." She handed over the case for her inspection.

"Yes, it's mine."

"You're quite sure?"

"Of course, I am," Mrs. Brownell retorted impatiently. "See, I'll show you." She opened the lid, displaying the picture. "This is a photo of my little girl, only it has been ruined."

Carson Drew and Nancy emerged from the closet and confronted the two startled women.

"Your identification is very interesting, Mrs. Brownell," the lawyer said evenly, "for that compact is stolen property."

"What do you mean?" she gasped, backing away.

"The jeweled case no doubt was given to you by a member of a notorious smuggling ring," the lawyer said quietly, "as a reward for your past services in selling stolen jewelry for them."

Mrs. Brownell stared hard at Mr. Drew and knew that his words were no idle bluff. She suddenly darted toward the door. But the lawyer, prepared for such a move, caught her firmly by the wrists. Simultaneously two federal agents appeared in the doorway to block Mrs. Cartlett's escape.

After Mrs. Brownell had been informed of her constitutional rights, Mr. Drew urged her to tell the truth. "If you turn state's evidence your prison term probably will be lighter."

"It's true—the compact is stolen property," the accused woman admitted after a long moment of silence. "I didn't mean to steal nor to have dealings with thieves, but I met a very pleasant man who induced me to help him. At first I thought it was honest work, and I accepted this jeweled compact in payment.

"Later on I was rewarded with other rich presents, including another valuable compact to replace the one I lost. I put another picture of my daughter in it." She paused before adding, "By the time I suspected the truth there was no retreating. Many times I tried to break away from the gang, but it was impossible."

"What are the names of these persons with whom you have been dealing?"

Mrs. Brownell's eyes roved accusingly toward her companion.

"You can't drag me into this!" the other woman cried out.

Carson Drew looked at her intently. "As soon as I heard Miss Judson's story and learned your name and where you were staying, I contacted the authorities in New York. Your past record is known. Our case against you is very damaging, even without Mrs. Brownell's testimony."

"I will tell everything," Mrs. Brownell promised, "but only upon one condition."

"What is that?" the lawyer asked.

"My little daughter must not be involved in this sordid mess. She is attending school in Paris and knows nothing about it. May I please have her picture back?"

"I'll do my best to keep the knowledge of your arrest from her," Mr. Drew promised as he handed over the photograph.

"I will gladly make a full confession," Mrs. Brownell agreed, "without the advice of counsel."

The woman named all the members of the ring of jewel thieves including Mrs. Cartlett. She agreed to dictate the confession later and sign it.

"One more question," said Mr. Drew. "Did you burn down the Judson mansion?"

"No, no, I had nothing to do with that! The fire was an accident."

"But you did visit Miss Judson with the intention of stealing the family jewels?"

"Yes, I deliberately brought up the subject with her, inducing her to open the safe. When she wasn't looking, I took a valuable necklace, a ruby pin, and a diamond-studded watch. Miss Judson carried the other jewels to her room."

"What became of the stolen articles?"

"I pawned them and gave part of the money to the gang."

"Do you still have the tickets?" Margaret Judson asked eagerly.

"Yes, I kept them because the jewels were worth far more than I received from the pawnbroker."

Margaret Judson was overjoyed to learn that every piece of her missing property would be returned. After federal agents had taken away the two prisoners, she thanked Nancy and Mr. Drew for their kindness.

"In helping you we helped ourselves," the lawyer replied. "Mrs. Brownell's confession is the beginning of the end for the ring of thieves."

"I think we are all rather surprised that Martin Bartescue had nothing to do with jewel smuggling," Nancy commented.

Her father smiled. "Apparently he's just a boaster."

Soon after the departure of the federal agents and the prisoners, Mark Wardell, Bess, George, and the three boys appeared at the cabin. They had remained away because they did not want to hamper the work of the detectives. There was general rejoicing because Margaret Judson had been completely vindicated.

"One angle of the mystery baffles me," Nancy declared as they all sat grouped about Joe Haley's bed. "I keep wondering who set up the scarecrow that made the bridge seem haunted."

Mr. Haley, who had enjoyed listening to the account of the day's happenings, began to chuckle.

"I did it," he announced. "Inquisitive young campers kept coming here and causing trouble. They bothered my mountain lion and tramped on my flowers. I thought the scarecrow might help to keep people away.

"It kept dogs away too. They used to attack the figure and bark so loudly that I'd always hear them and drive them off before they could come up here and damage my choice plants."

"Is that why you ran away from me?" Nancy asked. "Because you didn't want visitors?"

Mr. Haley nodded. "I didn't want anybody here, but now I'm glad to have friends like you."

Burt spoke up. "When Dave and I repaired the bridge, we set a new scarecrow in place. He'll guard your property for a long time to come."

"There's still one more thing to be explained," Bess declared. "What caused the groaning noise we heard so often?"

"I know the answer." Nancy smiled. "Wait until we walk over the haunted bridge on our way back to the hotel." She winked at Mr. Haley and whispered to him. He nodded.

Margaret Judson planned to remain with her former gardener and care for him until he could resume his usual duties. Ned, Burt, and Dave were no longer needed.

Mr. Haley grinned. "Now you'll be free to enjoy several days of fun before you return home."

Ned winked at the elderly man. "How long do you think Nancy Drew can just have fun? Only until the next mystery comes along—say in three days?"

Nancy chuckled. "Mysteries are fun too. Be sure all of you are around to help solve the next one."

Ned's prediction was almost right. Within a couple of weeks Nancy and her friends found themselves deeply involved in another intriguing case, *The Clue of the Tapping Heels*.

As the young people prepared to leave the cabin, Margaret Judson took the girls aside to tell them that she and Mark Wardell planned to be married as soon as Mr. Haley was better, so he could attend.

"Mark and I expect to rebuild the old mansion," she revealed. "Joe Haley has promised to take care of the property for us, and we hope to reestablish everything just as it was before the fire."

"Wonderful!" said Nancy, and the other girls echoed her good wishes.

On the way back to the hotel, everyone talked excitedly about the happy outcome of the mystery. When they reached the middle of the footbridge, Nancy called Bess's attention to two tall trees.

"There's the cause of the spooky sound we heard so often."

"I don't see—" Bess began, then trailed off into silence.

The wind was rocking the treetops, and as two thick boughs rubbed together, the strange moaning and groaning could be heard.

"Nancy, you're the greatest," George declared.

No matter how many mysteries Nancy had solved, her friends never ceased to be amazed each time.

Single file, the group trudged across the bridge, a little sorry their adventure had ended. But there was laughter when Nancy, who came last, paused to shake one limp arm of the flapping scarecrow.

"Good-by, old Mr. Ghost!" she addressed him gaily. "A million thanks for spooking me into a very puzzling mystery."

DETACH ALONG DOTTED LINE AND MAIL IN ENVELOPE WITH PAYMENT